THE ACCIDENT

Gillian Jackson

SAPERE
BOOKS

THE ACCIDENT

Published by Sapere Books.

20 Windermere Drive, Leeds, England, LS17 7UZ,
United Kingdom

saperebooks.com

ISBN: 978-1-913335-95-3

ACKNOWLEDGEMENTS

Many thanks to Denise Smith, a truly inspirational lady, whose generous help and advice enabled me to create the character of Hannah. Also to the amazing team at Sapere Books who work so hard on my behalf and from whom I continue to learn so much on my journey as an author.

CHAPTER 1

The day that changed everything for Hannah Graham began in exactly the same way as any other. Not unusually, she overslept, showered at record speed and shouted at her kids at least three times before either of them took any notice. Her daughter Mel's eventual response was to slam the bathroom door and her son Sam shouted an obscenity which he knew his mother hated him to use.

'If you want a lift you need to be ready in twenty minutes!' Hannah yelled up the stairs.

Sam stomped into the kitchen in his boxers, reddish-brown hair mussed above a scowling face. At seventeen, he was at an age where he appeared to be all arms and legs protruding from a skinny body, with features which he'd not quite grown into yet. He'd also recently been afflicted by acne, which he hated anyone mentioning.

'Mel's got in the bathroom before me again — she'll be ages!' he moaned. 'Why can't you wake me first?'

'Why can't you get up the first time I call you and then you'll get there before your sister?' Hannah replied. 'You can use our en suite if you like?'

'But all my stuff's in that bathroom!'

'Well, have some breakfast while you wait. If you want a lift this morning I need to be prompt — there's an early meeting at work.' Hannah placed a cup of coffee in front of him.

'There's not a lecture until eleven, so I'm good.' Sam poured cereal into the bowl his mother passed him. 'Is Dad not home yet?'

'No. He rang to say he couldn't make it last night — there are miles of roadworks on the M6 and the forecast's not good, so he decided to stay over until today.'

Hannah's husband, Mike, worked in sales and seemed to be constantly on the road, staying away for up to four nights at a time, on an all too regular basis. It was certainly not ideal in the kind of weather they were currently experiencing, and caused Hannah to worry for his safety. She hated him being away but had long since ceased to argue with him over the hours he worked. It was true that at almost eighteen the twins were of an age where they were capable of looking after themselves, but she still maintained that his unsocial hours had a negative effect on their family life.

'What family life?' Mike would argue. 'They're teenagers; they don't want to be around us!'

Hannah suspected that it was really her husband who didn't want to be around them, or maybe it was just her he wished to avoid? Perhaps it was natural for them all to do their own thing, but she was sadly aware that Mel and Sam would be going off to university in a few months' time, and what kind of life would she and Mike have then? She supposed her work would take on greater importance. She did love her job as office manager at a large estate agents, but when the twins were gone, there could be precious little else left.

Increasingly, she anticipated their leaving with mixed feelings; frustrating though they were at times, she adored having them at home, and knew she'd miss them terribly. On the other hand, she secretly nursed the hope that when there was just her and Mike, they would be able to recapture some of the sparkle which had escaped their marriage over the years. In her heart she hoped that perhaps, if they devoted more time to each other, things might improve between them. Maybe they could even travel to some of those exotic places they used to dream about before the children came along, but while Mike was working such long hours, it seemed unlikely that this would ever happen.

Hannah hadn't always been stuck in the rut of domesticity. After she and Mike married they'd made plans and promises, determined that whatever life threw their way they would always appreciate each other and the joy they shared. Midnight picnics, impromptu snowball fights and surprise gifts were just some of the little things which kept their relationship spontaneous, and laughter had always filled their home. There was no reason to think that life would ever be any different.

When the twins came along naturally things changed, but Hannah tried hard to keep the romance alive in her marriage, even throughout the constant exhaustion of those early years. Exactly when things began to change she couldn't quite pinpoint, yet she still thought of their life as being good; they were financially stable with a healthy family and Hannah was always one to count her blessings. The magic of those early days had simply matured into something different; a contentment perhaps? Yes, that's what it was for her, contentment, and for Mike too, she hoped.

'Mel!' she shouted up the stairs. 'Do you want a lift this morning? I'm leaving in ten minutes!'

'No, I'm not in until lunch!' her daughter shouted down the stairs.

Honestly, they were hardly ever at the sixth form college — Hannah didn't know how they'd get the required grades for university when they didn't seem to do any work. Still, they were old enough to know what they were doing — or were supposed to be.

Mel almost ran into the kitchen as Hannah was pulling her coat on. She was a pretty girl with her mother's rich auburn hair framing a well-proportioned face, high cheekbones and lively green eyes. Mike used to say their daughter was the image of Hannah as she'd been when they first met.

'Can you leave me twenty pounds, Mum?' she asked. 'I need some new mascara.'

'You're not going to pay that much just for mascara, are you?'

Mel rolled her eyes, an all too common expression which made Hannah smile; she'd perfected precisely the same eye roll for her own mother's benefit when she was a teenager, and knew exactly what her daughter was thinking.

'No, the mascara's only twelve, but I need some money to get the bus into town.'

'What happened to your allowance?' Hannah was already fishing in her bag for her purse, knowing that her daughter went through money like it was going out of fashion.

Mel tutted. 'My allowance is barely enough to last the week.' She took the twenty pound note almost before her mother pulled it from her purse. 'Thanks, Mum!'

Hannah checked the time and hurried to the door, her parting remark being a mundane reminder: 'Remember to stack the dishwasher before you leave.'

Outside, the atrocious weather hadn't improved, the snow was now tightly packed onto the roads, the temperature barely reaching zero, and freezing rain was beginning to fall. It looked as if the gritting lorry hadn't made it again either; the council was quickly running out of salt for the roads. 'The Beast from the East' they were calling it, which seemed a spot-on description to Hannah; she couldn't ever remember a colder start to February. The wind was biting cold, chilling her to the bone even though she'd only just left the warmth of the house.

Rosie, her neighbour and best friend, was also leaving for work.

'You still on for tonight, Hannah?' she called out.

Hannah stopped suddenly; she'd completely forgotten that she'd agreed to a girls' night out with Rosie and a couple of their other friends.

'Oh, sorry but I'll have to pass on this one. Mike didn't get back last night so I can hardly go out and leave him when he hasn't been home for three nights.'

'Why not? He's big enough to look after himself!' Rosie was obviously disappointed.

'Next time, Rosie, promise! Anyway, it's hardly fit to venture out unless you have to.'

Hannah hurried to the garage to get out of the freezing rain, clutching her coat to her neck against the bitter cold, and reversed the car out, feeling bad at letting her friend down.

On a good day it took twenty minutes for Hannah to get to the office — on a bad one, nearer forty. This morning she hoped for light traffic, although the icy roads would probably slow things down considerably. Driving carefully towards the motorway, Hannah's thoughts again turned to Mike. Their twentieth wedding anniversary was coming up soon; should she surprise him by booking a holiday? But then his reaction might not be what she hoped for, and the problem he would have getting time off work would undoubtedly cause more arguments between them.

It seemed that the longer Mike had been with the company, the more they expected of him, but apparently Hannah minded more than he did. It appeared to her that the firm took advantage of her husband, and even on his rest days there were calls at short notice, expecting him to drop everything and go wherever they deigned to send him.

In the last month Mike had been away more nights than he'd been at home, which was hardly a recipe for a healthy relationship. Hannah wished he'd assert himself more and say no to his boss, rather than so willingly jumping every time they said 'go'.

The traffic was heavier than Hannah had expected and every traffic light seemed to be against her — always the same when you were running late, she thought. The reason for the early meeting was to discuss a potential merger with another local estate agent, and Hannah's thoughts switched to the possibility. The merger could certainly offer the chance of promotion for her, or even a partnership in time, but that inevitably meant extra responsibility, and did she really want that?

If only Mike had come home last night they could have talked it through before the meeting this morning; she would have appreciated his opinion on it. Niggling at the back of her mind was the thought that if Mike didn't cut down on his nights away, when the time came for the twins to leave for university, she'd most probably welcome the extra work.

She missed having her husband around to talk to and didn't really know what he wanted out of life anymore. Mike seemed content to drift along, rudderless, with no thought to their immediate or long term future. How could she be expected to make decisions when he was never there to discuss them with?

There was a queue on the motorway slip road that would probably cost her another five minutes. With such atrocious weather it would have been a perfect day for staying at home. Hannah was due some leave, but the meeting was crucial and she needed to be there. The local schools had been closed for the last three days, but a few days at home wasn't to be for her, and like most other people she braved the cold and made every effort to get into work.

The other vehicles joining the motorway were mostly heavy goods traffic; Hannah was behind two lorries and would most likely be flanked by others when she eventually joined the motorway. Snow was piled high at both sides of the road and the freezing rain lashed violently onto the windscreen, as if trying to get inside the car, making her shudder. It sounded like bullets rapping on the roof.

Hannah hated this drive, but there was no alternative route without adding an extra eleven miles and a further twenty minutes to the journey, so she suffered the motorway traffic every day.

The line of traffic began to move — a few stop-starts, then the road ahead cleared a little and she could see a gap coming up on the motorway. Slipping into first, then second gear, Hannah moved carefully forward, willing the gap to stay open long enough for her to slot into it and join the motorway traffic.

But the next thing she knew her car seemed to take on a mind of its own; she lost control as the wheels skidded on the ice and the car veered forward, first to the right and then the left.

Hannah felt panic rising inside her, catching in her throat until she could hardly breathe; she was utterly helpless as the car gathered momentum down the slope of the slip road. Suddenly, her Ford Focus spun 180 degrees, with no possible way for her to avoid the back end of the car from smashing into the enormous rear wheel of the lorry which was moving towards her at speed on the motorway.

The little car was instantly filled with noise, horrendous grating noise, which she recognised as the sound of crushing metal, as it came to a sudden, violent halt. Her head was thrown backwards and as she stared helplessly out of the front windscreen, Hannah was momentarily aware of a dark-coloured Range Rover heading straight towards her, the impending impact frighteningly unavoidable. For a split second she made eye contact with the male driver whose face mirrored her own horror at what was happening and at what they were both powerless to prevent.

Hannah briefly took in the frightened expression of the woman sitting next to him before she heard herself scream, but the sound seemed to come from somewhere outside of the car, an echo of sheer panic, raw fear, before darkness and pain enveloped everything and her world went black.

CHAPTER 2

Joe Parker was convinced he was going through a mid-life crisis; he despaired as to whether this was it, the slippery slope to old age and then ... the inevitable, the big 'D'. Looking in the mirror scared him these days, but he couldn't resist studying his face, wondering what had happened to his once firm jawline and taut skin. The reflection staring back at him was that of a much older man whom he barely recognised.

Joe was only forty-three but, like the camera, he supposed the mirror didn't lie. Loose skin sagged from his jaws and bags had appeared beneath his eyes; his skin was sallow too, with an unhealthy yellow tinge to it. Could it be the cigarettes? He'd tried so many times to kick the habit but his resolve crumbled after only a matter of days. The booze wouldn't help either; he had a penchant for fine whisky and fancied himself as a bit of a wine buff, but he liked to think he kept his drinking in moderation.

Joe wasn't stupid, he knew the detrimental effect these things had on a person's body yet he'd never considered that it would happen to him. He'd always enjoyed a smoke and a few drinks without seriously thinking of the damage they were doing to his body. His hair was definitely thinning as well, although he knew much younger men who would be glad to have the amount of hair he still had.

There was his mind too; Joe was certain that he was slowing down mentally. Only a couple of days before he'd been talking to someone in the pub, not a close friend, but another regular whom he'd known to pass the time of day with for several years, and he couldn't remember the man's name. After a three-minute conversation the name still wouldn't come to mind, and he'd left the pub that night frustrated and wondering if he was finally losing it.

Morning sounds from the kitchen were rising up the stairs and Joe realised he'd better get a move on. In the kitchen Alison, his wife, made him toast and coffee, the same breakfast he ate every day, while she nibbled on fruit and yoghurt.

'You all right this morning, love?' she asked. 'You're looking a bit down in the mouth.'

'Yes, I'm fine. Didn't sleep too well, that's all. Have you taken Liffey out yet?'

'Yes, we've had a quick walk through the meadow but it's absolutely freezing — we were both ready to get back home. You haven't forgotten that you're dropping me at Mum's this morning, have you?'

'No, of course not,' Joe lied as he spread a generous helping of butter on his toast. He could have done without the detour on his way to work, especially in this weather, but at least if Alison went to visit her mum today he wouldn't be expected to take her at the weekend. *Every cloud*, he thought.

While his wife washed up the breakfast things Joe went back upstairs to brush his teeth. He studied the yellowing teeth which had once been white and even. *I don't know why she stays with me*, he thought. Alison was still trim and pretty at forty-two, but then she worked hard to keep her figure, with Pilates and swimming, and a healthy diet. Was it too late for him? he wondered, knowing that he was basically too lazy to put in the effort. His waistline had thickened considerably in the last few years but Alison was great, never nagging him about it although he knew she harboured concerns about his health. Alison was the bright spot in his life, his 'reason for living' he called her; corny, he knew.

'Come on, love!' Joe called to his wife ten minutes later. 'We don't want to keep your mum waiting.'

She held on to his arm as they negotiated the icy path leading to the garage.

'I've never known such a long cold snap,' Alison grumbled.

Once they were in the car and the heater began to warm them through, Joe asked, 'Do you think I should try to eat a little more healthily, Ali?'

'I think that's a great idea.' She smiled. 'I'm sure you'd like some of those recipes I get from the slimming magazines. We could both make an effort, work at it together.'

Nothing more was said and Joe knew that his wife would go about helping him in her own quiet way; she was great like that and, in all honesty, deserved better than him. Perhaps he'd even have another go at giving up smoking, for both their sakes.

They'd been married now for eighteen years, most of which had been blissfully happy. Their one big regret was that they hadn't been blessed with children, but as with every other setback in life, Alison simply got on with it without complaint — the painful subject was barely referred to anymore now that it was too late and the chance had passed them by for good. They'd briefly looked into the possibility of adoption but the lengthy process seemed so fraught with problems and red tape that they soon abandoned the idea, and then, five years ago, they'd decided to get a dog. Neither of them was naive enough to think that a dog could ever be the same as a child, but they had love to give, a good home, and plenty of time and patience, so after a visit to the local animal sanctuary, Liffey came into their lives. They fell in love with her as soon as they laid eyes on her sweet face, beautiful rich golden coat and large velvet brown eyes.

'She was found abandoned on the streets of Ireland, frightened and hungry,' the manager had told them. 'We think she's part golden Labrador, crossed perhaps with a Lurcher.'

Liffey had only been at the centre for a couple of days and hadn't settled well at all. Alison was horrified to see that the poor dog had blood on her paws.

'What's happened to her?' she had asked.

'She can't take to kennel life, I'm afraid; she barked and scratched through most of the night. If you were interested in her we'd really want you to take her as soon as possible.'

Alison and Joe had exchanged glances. There was no doubt that they wanted this dog — in fact they would find it very difficult to leave without her. She'd been named Sugar, but Joe suggested Liffey as a reminder of her Irish roots, and so Liffey she became, and very quickly took centre stage in their household.

Slim for a Labrador, which was probably the Lurcher in her, they soon found out that Liffey had issues. At first she was very nervous — they even wondered at times if she'd ever lived in a house before — but settling her in became a welcome focus for Alison and Joe, and over the first year she became an important part of their lives and they doted on her. Joe liked to joke that he had two women in the house bossing him around now, but he loved every minute of it.

Not having children meant that money wasn't tight for the Parkers like it was for many of their friends with families, and they weren't tied in any way. They'd taken some memorable, perhaps some would say extravagant, holidays and been able to go to places they would never have afforded if they had a family.

Still, Joe knew that Alison would really have loved a child ... and so would he — holidays could never compensate for that loss. He'd been thinking about their childless status a lot lately. He worried about who would look after Ali when he was gone. True, she was an intelligent, capable woman, but he'd always taken delight in caring for her.

The traffic was slow and dropping Alison off would mean Joe would be late getting into work, but he was the department head and there would certainly be no one waiting to reprimand him for tardiness. His thoughts turned to his mother-in-law, a woman he found very difficult to get along with. Alison went faithfully twice a week, often more, to do her cleaning, washing, ironing, and shopping. He didn't mind, except that the old lady didn't appreciate it one iota, and the more Alison did for her, the more she expected, without ever expressing a word of gratitude. She sat watching television from early morning until late at night, not attempting to do anything for herself, when she was more than capable of making the effort.

Joe drove carefully, never one to take risks, and with the roads still covered in ice from the cold snap of the last week, he wasn't going to hurry. There was no let-up in this abysmal weather; he couldn't remember it ever being as bad as this and his wipers struggled to clear the freezing rain which was falling heavily, making visibility poor. Once on the motorway the conditions would hopefully be a little better and as they were approaching the slip road soon, he should be able to go a little faster. His Range Rover was great in these conditions, another luxury which he should be grateful for, and very soon he manoeuvred smoothly into the flow of traffic on the motorway with only two miles to go until the next junction.

'Shall we eat out tonight, Joe?' Alison asked him. 'If I stay at Mum's until you finish work you can pick me up and we could go straight to The Mango Tree?'

'Yes, why not, a last splurge before you put me on a diet — What the hell!'

Joe was forced to brake hard as a little Ford Focus careering down the slip road ahead of them came into his vision, apparently having skidded on the ice and now obviously out of control. He watched in horror as its wheels slid onto the motorway, the car spinning round and ending up with its back end smashed into a lorry which was approaching on the near side.

Suddenly, he felt his own car slide beneath him. Panicking, he pumped the brakes frantically but the tires couldn't find purchase on the ice beneath them and they were heading towards the stricken Ford Focus, helpless to prevent the impending contact. An image of a screaming woman loomed in his windscreen, as if magnified, but he was powerless to stop his car from hitting hers, head on.

Alison screamed as the air bags activated on impact, obscuring their view as they smashed into the other car. Joe's ears were filled with white noise as he gasped for breath, struggling against the fabric of the air bag and shouting at his wife.

'Ali, are you all right? Ali, Ali!'

There was no reply.

The car was jolted several times, grating noises assaulting his ears as he realised that other vehicles must have crashed into the back of them. Joe fought frantically against the air bag in an effort to get out of the door, but it wouldn't open. The front wing had buckled on impact and the door was jammed.

Clawing at the air bag, he managed to pull the voluminous folds of material down onto his knee until he could see his wife. Alison lay unconscious beside him, her head slack and drooping onto her right shoulder, a trickle of blood running from her mouth. A feeling of utter helplessness engulfed him as he reached over to touch her, grasping for her hand as he repeated her name over and over.

The windscreen was shattered, preventing him from seeing out of it and his neck hurt, with a stabbing pain shooting into his head and down through his arm as he tried to look out of the side window. Noises from outside seeped into the car, the grating and grinding sounds of metal, followed by screams, shouting and sobbing and the constant rhythmic drumming of the heavy, icy rain, pounding on the roof of the car.

Joe had no idea how many cars were now stationary, caught up in the tangled web of metal which only moments ago were individual vehicles. Tears ran down his face as he waited, utterly powerless to do anything to help himself, or his wife. It seemed like an eternity until he heard sirens in the distance and he began to pray that they would get to Alison in time.

His eyes struggled to focus and his head swam. Joe wanted nothing more than to close his eyes and drift away into unconsciousness, but he knew he must keep awake for Alison. *Talk to her*, he told himself, *keep her with you!*

'Alison... Ali, can you hear me, love?'

There was silence, not a groan or a sob, just the most frightening silence inside the car, not even the sound of breathing, while outside the noise was building. Suddenly someone was trying to open his side door, a fireman, suited up in black overalls.

'My wife!' Joe cried. 'My wife needs help, please!'

The door opened with a sudden jerk and a strong arm reached in to help him out.

'Leave me, get Alison please ... she's unconscious!'

'It's okay, my colleague's working on getting her out now. Let's get you to safety though, shall we?'

21

Joe's legs threatened to buckle beneath him as he was led towards the snow-covered verge. He was in tremendous pain and unable to turn his head to see what was happening back at his car. His body trembled with the cold and an even colder fear. 'Is she all right? My wife, Alison, is she all right?'

He was becoming increasingly light-headed and almost collapsed into the fireman's arms, the acrid smell of burnt rubber making him feel nauseous. The next thing he knew he was inside an ambulance, wrapped in a silver foil blanket with his neck supported by a huge, uncomfortable collar. His eyes tried to stay open but it was such an effort.

'Hi, mate, can you tell me your name?'

Joe was aware of the figure of a man beside him, talking to him, asking him questions.

'How's my wife ... Alison?' He wasn't sure if he'd got the words right but the man beside him patted his arm.

'We're almost at the hospital now; your wife will either be there already or be arriving shortly. Can you tell me your name?'

'Joe, Joe Parker.'

'Well, you're doing fine, Joe. No broken limbs but there could be a problem with your collarbone. They'll check you out properly when we get to the hospital; an X-ray should show up any breaks. '

Joe closed his eyes again, tears escaping unchecked, he didn't care about himself, all he could think about was Alison.

'Stay awake if you can, mate. Tell me where you were going, can you?' The man's voice was quiet and even, but persistent. Joe didn't want to talk, he wanted to sleep, to wake up and find that this had all been a nightmare. He wanted to see Alison, to make sure she was all right — she had to be all right. Joe couldn't make it without her.

CHAPTER 3

The death of a child is never easy; it is not the natural order of the world and leaves a void which can never be filled. Timothy Jones was just fifteen and an only child when he left behind his devastated parents, three grandparents and other extended family, all of whom loved Timmy dearly and would always feel the gaping hole left by his premature death. He'd been so full of life and love, touching the hearts of everyone he came into contact with, but it seemed that he was only on loan to his family and even that was for such a short time, far too short.

When Timothy was conceived in 2003, an extra chromosome in the baby's cells caused him to develop Down's syndrome, just one of almost 800 babies who are born with Down's syndrome in England and Wales each year.

Cassie Jones was only twenty-eight when the results of a test in early pregnancy flagged up the potential risk of having a baby with Down's syndrome, and she was advised to have an amniocentesis test. Her response was immediate and negative. It was an invasive procedure, involving risk to the baby as fluid was taken from the womb to be tested, but the risk wasn't Cassie's primary reason for refusing the test. If her baby had Down's syndrome it would make no difference whatsoever to her and Alan, her husband. They had planned this baby; he was made up of a little part of each of them and therefore loved and wanted from that very moment of conception, even before. There was no way they would even consider an abortion, so the test was unnecessary.

As their baby grew in her womb, so did his parents' love, unwavering, unshakable and strong. The birth was as exciting and special as every other birth, and when Timothy was placed into his mother's arms for the first time, her body flooded with love as she gazed into the tiny crumpled features of her perfect son. Down's syndrome would not define Timmy any more than having brown eyes would, and his parents looked upon him as a gift from God.

There were whispers on the maternity ward and sympathetic looks. Cassie felt sorry for those other mothers. Was what they perceived as perfection the only criteria for a healthy child, for being a happy, fulfilled family? The difficulties the Jones's faced as parents in the years to come might not be so very different, or more onerous, than those these other parents faced. Who was able to predict what lay ahead, or to define what a 'normal' child was?

Timothy brought his parents fifteen years of joy. Fifteen years of laughter and sunshine — tears too of course, but how can you appreciate the light without the darkness? On Friday 2nd February, 2018, Timothy's school had been closed for the third consecutive day due to the awful weather and the boy had been bored. He loved school and became frustrated and antsy when he couldn't attend. His parents had fought hard for his place at their local mainstream school, where their son's achievements surpassed all expectations and Timothy was a popular, hard-working pupil.

It was also the morning of his orthodontist appointment and Alan Jones considered cancelling this too, due to the atrocious weather, but relented to his son's pleadings and decided to go ahead with the appointment, to give Timothy some relief from yet another day confined to home.

Alan, a veterinary surgeon, had an evening surgery at his practice and so, being free that morning, elected to take his son to the appointment himself, rather than letting Cassie drive in the snow.

Alan would always regret his decision to attend that appointment, one which changed their lives and robbed them of their precious only child. One of the hardest things for Alan to come to terms with was that he had walked away from the accident with only a slight graze to his forehead and a sprained wrist. Why couldn't he have sustained the greater injuries and his son be spared? Surely Alan didn't deserve to come out of it with barely a scratch, when Timothy lost his life?

The emotional pain simply wasn't enough, Alan wanted to feel physical pain too, he felt he deserved to feel it, he needed to feel it. Cassie too was haunted, wishing she had stopped her husband and son from going that day, wishing she'd been with them and then it would have been her in the front seat of the car and she might have survived the impact. The couple comforted each other in the best way they could, but Timmy's laughing, loving, huge presence left an ache, an enormous vacuum in their lives, one which they had no idea how to fill.

CHAPTER 4

Hannah began to wake. Awareness of being in a strange place made her think she was still dreaming. Her head ached, her arms felt stiff and she could feel a searing pain throughout most of her body as she struggled to open her eyes. Someone had hold of her hand, squeezing it gently and talking to her; he was repeating her name.

'Hannah... Hannah, can you hear me?'

It was Mike. She recognised his voice and smiled, but her mouth was sore, her lip felt crusted, and cracked painfully with the movement, her mouth suddenly filled with that awful metallic taste of blood. What was going on? She tried again to open her eyes and saw her husband, sitting on a chair beside a bed, a hospital bed, but why was she in hospital? She tried to turn her head, to ask what was going on but her body was being strangely uncooperative.

'Mike.' Her voice was hoarse, raspy. 'What's happening?'

'It's all right, love. You were in a car accident and you're in hospital now. Don't worry, you're okay and I'm here.'

Her husband stood over her and she could see the anguish in his face — his eyes were watery and red.

'But I can't remember.' Hannah felt panic rising inside her. How could she have been in an accident and not remember?

'That's okay. The doctor said you might not remember the accident for a while, but it'll probably come back to you. It's not important now.' He stroked her forehead, pushing a lock of hair behind her ears.

'What happened? Where was I going? Were the children with me?' The sudden thought alarmed her and she silently prayed that the twins were okay.

'They're both fine, and no they weren't with you in the car. You were alone. Don't worry about it now; we can fill you in on the details later.'

Mike forced a smile and she could tell he was trying to reassure her but he was obviously worried, she could always tell when he was worried by the little twitch at the corner of his mouth.

Hannah asked nothing more; it was enough to concentrate on breathing and keeping her eyes open, she was so tired and even these simple tasks were an effort. The pain was nauseating. She could tell her face was swollen and her eyes wouldn't open fully.

Mike reached over the bed and pressed the call button for the nurse.

'I'm all right,' she said. 'Just tired.' Hannah was aware of tubes in her arms and one of those cages over her legs. 'Have I got a broken leg?' she asked.

'No, love ... here's the nurse — she'll want to see how you are.'

Mike took a step back from the bed and a rather too cheery nurse approached and took hold of her hand.

'Hello, Hannah, how are you feeling?'

'Groggy. My head's pounding and my neck's stiff. I'm in a lot of pain too.'

'That's to be expected. When the doctor's seen you we can look at increasing the pain meds. You took quite a battering in the accident. There are a few cuts and bruises on your face and head but they'll heal.' As she spoke the nurse began to take Hannah's blood pressure and clipped something like a bulldog clip onto her finger. 'All good,' she smiled. 'Doctor will be round soon but try to rest; we can always wake you again when he comes.'

As she moved away from the bed Mike followed her and when they were out of Hannah's earshot they exchanged a few whispered words.

'What was all that about?' Hannah asked when he came back to her side.

'Nothing really. Look, I'm going to ring the kids to let them know you're awake. Rest if you can, I won't be long.'

'Why do they need to know that — how long have I been asleep?' She studied Mike's worried expression, trying to read what was in his mind.

'You've been in an induced coma, love, for three days.'

'Three days! What day is it now, and why an induced coma?' Hannah's mind was muddled; why did they keep people in an induced coma? She couldn't think straight.

'Shh, don't get yourself upset. I'll ring the kids and they can come in to see you this evening. They've been in a couple of times already, but now you're awake they'll be keen to come again.'

Before there was a chance to protest, Mike had gone. Hannah closed her eyes and drifted back into sleep.

'Do you want to tell her?' A man's quiet voice interrupted the sanctuary of sleep.

'I'd rather you did.'

That was Mike. Hannah opened her eyes, wondering if the children were with him. They weren't and the curtains were drawn around her bed.

'Tell me what?' She looked at the solemn faces of her husband and the man beside him, presumably a doctor, and panic gripped her.

'Hello, Hannah.' The man smiled. 'I'm Dr Singh. I think your husband told you that you've been in an accident?' She nodded, willing him to get to the point. 'Well, your car was pretty badly damaged and the firemen had no alternative but to cut you out of the wreckage. When you arrived here you'd lost a lot of blood and the damage to your right leg was severe. Surgery was the only option. I'm afraid there was no way we could save your leg.'

Hannah felt her chest tighten as if someone was pressing down on her and hysteria threatened to take over. Struggling to sit up and look down at her legs, she lacked the strength to lift her head, and pain shot through her body.

The doctor put his hand on her shoulder and Mike held her hand.

'No!' She pushed against them. Hannah couldn't believe it, didn't want to believe it, but her voice wouldn't come, the words were strangled in sobs. Was he really telling her they'd cut off her leg?

'We amputated below your knee, which is the best possible outcome we could manage, so in time you'll be able to have a prosthetic limb fitted, which will mean that you'll be able to walk.' The doctor said this as if it was good news, as if she should be grateful.

'I want to see it,' Hannah managed to say.

'Perhaps it's best not to —' Mike began but she cut him off.

'I want to see!' She was emphatic, the panic turning rapidly to anger.

The doctor motioned to a nurse who was hovering in the background and she came to the top of the bed and began to help Hannah lift her head and shoulders.

'It's dressed, of course,' said the doctor, as he calmly pulled the covers back.

Hannah stared down at the huge mass of bandages where her right leg should have been, horrified at the sight. A plastic tube protruded from the bandages, draining into a bag at the side of the bed and there was a catheter from between her legs. It was so ugly … and so final.

A sound escaped from somewhere deep inside her, a muffled sob or gasp, when she really wanted to shout and scream. Tears blurred her vision as the nurse gently laid her back down.

'I know this is a shock now,' the doctor continued, 'but in time your body will adjust, and prosthetic limbs are amazing these days. I'll leave you with your husband now and if you've any questions I'll be back later this afternoon.'

He turned and left, followed by the nurse, as if they couldn't wait to get out of there. They'd imparted the awful news, done the difficult task and Mike was left alone with her, looking bewildered and awkward.

'My leg!' Hannah cried bitterly, the reality of what she'd been told, and what she'd seen for herself, was almost too painful to bear. Her husband's arms were suddenly around her and she clung to him as she sobbed, feeling Mike's own tears, warm against her face.

'I know, I know, it'll be all right…' he repeated.

Empty words, she thought, how could it be all right ever again?

A few minutes later a nurse peered through the curtains.

'I thought you might like this.' She carried a cup of tea and placed it on the table beside the bed, a cure for all ills. 'Do you need anything else?' She began to check the drips, touching and adjusting them very deliberately. 'This is the pain medication and you can self-administer it, see?' She showed Hannah the button to press which would release the morphine into her arm. 'How bad is the pain, on a scale of one to ten?'

'Nine, ten, I don't know...' Hannah sobbed.

The nurse pressed the button for her and almost instantly Hannah felt the medication flowing through her body.

'It works pretty fast so don't use it too much but it's quite safe, you can't overdose on it, although too much might make you feel nauseous.' The nurse smiled; she looked so young, not very much older than Mel. 'If you need anything else just press the buzzer.'

Her calm efficiency had the effect of settling Hannah down, or was it the morphine? The sobs eased and she gulped in a few deep breaths. Feeling quite light-headed now she lay back on the pillows, but a wave of nausea swept over her and she tried to reach for the bowl at the bottom of the bed. Mike realised what was happening and passed it to her just in time. She retched, but there was nothing in her stomach.

When the feeling passed Hannah studied Mike, his face was as pale as her own. He'd never been good around illness of any kind, and she was surprised to find herself thinking about how he would cope with her disability, rather than how she would.

'Do the children know?' she asked.

'Yes. They'll be here any minute.'

As the twins entered the hospital ward Hannah forced a smile, pleased to see them but still numb from the knowledge of the extent of her injuries.

Mel almost threw herself on top of her mother, tears flowing unchecked.

'Oh, Mum, I'm so glad you're all right; we thought we'd lost you!'

Hannah was thankful for the cage protecting her legs, or what was left of them. Sam was quieter, kissing his mother on the cheek when his sister moved away; he could find no words to say but reached for her hand and squeezed it briefly.

'How've you been coping without me?' Hannah asked, trying to pretend everything was normal, while fearing that it never would be again.

'Okay,' Sam offered, not terribly convincingly.

'We've missed you of course, but we've managed, and Dad says he's not going to be going away again for a while, so we'll all be around to help when you come home.' Mel smiled, her intention so obviously to reassure her mother, but the words brought a chill to Hannah's heart. How much help would she need from her family and how readily could she accept it? She'd always been the one to do the caring, and loved the role, it didn't seem right that her husband and children would now have to look after her.

'I don't know how long I'll be in here,' she began to explain, 'but the doctor talked about a prosthetic leg. Maybe I'll have that fitted when I come home?' Really she'd not even considered the timescale of her recovery, but so desperately wanted to reassure her family, and possibly herself, that she wouldn't be a burden to them.

The conversation was strained and Hannah was visibly tiring. Mike made the decision that they would go home and let her sleep some more. Almost as a second thought he asked, 'Unless you'd like me to stay a little longer?'

'No, I think I need to sleep, but you'll all come again tomorrow?'

'Of course we will!' Mel spoke for them all before they kissed her goodbye, leaving her alone with a legion of troubled thoughts running through her mind.

CHAPTER 5

The doctor said that Joe had had a lucky escape. An X-ray revealed that his collarbone was broken, which was the cause of his pain — even trying to lift his head to drink made him wince. But in all honesty he felt anything but lucky and would much rather be dead, like his beloved Alison. His reason for living was gone, what did that mean for him now?

Alison hadn't deserved to die. It should have been him. She was so full of energy, a good person who loved life; he didn't, especially a life without Alison which stretched fearfully ahead of him, void of all happiness.

It had been over two hours before someone came to tell him that she was dead, two hours during which Joe asked and asked to the point of becoming a nuisance. At first they were too busy in Accident and Emergency for anyone to break off from tending the injured to enquire about his wife; the accident was declared a major incident and stretched the hospital's already strained and limited resources. He learned from listening to the nurses, that there were three fatalities, two women and a teenage boy, and positive identifications had to be made before informing the next of kin.

Joe was moved into a side ward where the chaplain, who'd obviously drawn the short straw, came with the ward sister to tell him that Alison was dead. The chaplain looked genuinely grieved to be bearing such news, his brow furrowed and his lips turned down at the corners as he placed his long slender fingers on Joe's good shoulder. His touch was cold, yet his words were warm, albeit hollow.

At first Joe refused to believe it; surely it was another woman who'd died, not his wife, it couldn't be her! But it was, and he wished with all his heart that it had been him instead of Alison.

The chaplain asked if there was anyone he wanted him to call, anyone who would come to be with him, but he could think of no one. Joe had a brother but they'd never been close and he lived somewhere on the south coast, he couldn't even remember the name of the town now. Alison's mother would need to be told; she'd wonder why her daughter hadn't arrived and would be unable to reach them on the phone.

The chaplain said he'd speak to one of the police officers and they would go round to break the news. It wasn't an ideal way for the old lady to hear that her daughter was dead, but Joe was in no fit state to go himself and as yet didn't know how long they'd keep him in hospital. He'd given the chaplain the address and also asked him to phone his neighbours for him, to ask them to look after Liffey.

Phil and Helen Roper had moved into the house next door to the Parkers ten years ago and the two couples hit it off from day one. They were of a similar age and although they didn't live in each other's pockets, both couples more than filled the role of 'good neighbours'. When Alison and Joe got Liffey, the friendship extended to dog-sitting. Phil had always wanted a dog but as he still worked and Helen had such a busy life, they felt it unfair to leave one at home all day, so they happily became sitters for Liffey and she was almost as comfortable in their home as her own. They readily looked after her when holidays came around and he knew that his dog would be fine with them.

Thinking about it now, he experienced a sudden longing for Liffey to be with him; her warm body and loving temperament would be a welcome comfort, perhaps she was the next most precious thing in his life ... after Ali.

Joe wondered if the other fatality was the woman in the Ford Focus into which his car had smashed. Surely if Alison hadn't survived the impact, the other woman would also be dead; her car must have been squashed to an unrecognisable mass. Would she leave a husband, and children?

Joe spent an uncomfortable night in the stuffy hospital ward. A nurse gave him painkillers but they couldn't ease the pain in his heart, the solid, painful, mass of emotion welling up in his chest at the thought of his wife, at the knowledge that he would never see her again, never hear her voice or touch her hand; it was unbearable.

Sleep refused to come, to afford him just a few hours respite, and in the darkness, tears fell readily. The neck brace he'd worn in the ambulance had been replaced with an arm sling, put on in such a way as to keep his arm immobilised so he could only lie on his back, which, even with pillows propping him up, was uncomfortable. Even without the pain and heavy sorrow he was experiencing, the unfamiliar night-time sounds of the busy ward would have been enough to keep him awake.

Dawn was almost a welcome relief and Joe forced himself to eat, wanting to build up his strength to enable him to go home as soon as possible.

A doctor appeared in his room later that morning, with the look of a man who hadn't slept, dark circles beneath his eyes, but his manner was professional and his voice soft and kind as he informed Joe that he could be discharged, but warned him to take his injuries seriously.

'Keep the sling on for the next two weeks. We'll do another X-ray then to make sure the bone is knitting together and hasn't moved. It's a bad break and will be swollen and quite painful for good while yet, so you must be careful not to use your arm. If the next X-ray's all right, you can begin some gentle exercise, but we'll talk about that when I see you again. I've written a prescription for some strong painkillers, they should help. I'm so sorry for your loss, Mr Parker. The ward sister has some leaflets which might be of interest to you.'

The doctor smiled sadly then left the room.

Joe knew he needed help to get dressed; he'd been unable to get to the bathroom earlier and much to his disgust had to use a bedpan. He didn't know how he was going to manage at home on his own, but he did know that he wanted to get out of the hospital as quickly as possible.

Just when he was thinking through the logistics of attempting to get dressed, the ward sister appeared and pulled the curtains around his bed. She held a bundle of leaflets in her hand and sat down on the chair by his bed.

'I know it's going to be difficult for you, Joe, but there is help out there if you want to take it.' She wasn't just talking about the practicalities of his injuries, and spread the leaflets on the bed. 'These are the contact details of a bereavement counselling service. They're very good and you can self-refer at any time just by ringing this number. We can also get in touch with social services to have someone come to the house for a week or two, to help you with getting a shower, or making meals, if you'd like that?'

Joe shuddered. The thought of a stranger coming in to help him shower was abhorrent. He'd manage somehow, he wasn't ancient and incapable yet. He politely declined and was given a number in case he changed his mind.

'Right, well I'll get your discharge letter and prescription ready now and a nurse will help you dress. Is there anyone I can phone to come and pick you up?'

Joe thought for a minute. 'What about Alison, my wife? I mean, I know her body's here and I'll have to arrange a funeral, but is there a death certificate or something that I need?'

A look of sadness crossed the ward sister's face. 'I'm sorry, Joe, but Alison will have to stay here for the time being.' She sat on the edge of the bed next to him and began to explain. 'After a fatal accident like this the coroner becomes involved to determine exactly what happened and there'll have to be an inquest. The death can't be registered until after that, and so Alison's body won't be released for a funeral until then either. What we can do, is to give you the medical certificate of death for you to take to the coroner, who'll then issue an interim death certificate, so you'll be able to notify the banks and places like that.'

Joe was stunned; he'd assumed that he'd be able to arrange the funeral almost immediately and now it looked as if it was going to be a long, drawn-out process. He gathered his thoughts and remembered the sister's earlier question.

'Sorry, that's come as a bit of a surprise, it's not what I was expecting. Could you ring my neighbour for me? If there's no answer I'll get a taxi.' He recited the number.

The ward sister nodded then smiled as she left him. They must see all sorts, he thought, surely he wasn't the only one who was ignorant of procedure ... and had no one to take him home.

Joe's clothes were in an appalling condition but unless he went home in a hospital gown he had no choice but to put them on. His wallet was still in the inside pocket of his jacket so at least he'd have some money to pay for a taxi if it was necessary, and someone had had the forethought to put his keys in the pocket too.

There were dark stains on his left-hand jacket sleeve. In the deepest recesses of his mind, Joe knew it was Alison's blood but he refused to think about it, except to make the decision to burn all the clothes he'd been wearing yesterday when he got home. The events of the previous day seemed to be embedded into their very fabric; each fibre held the smell of burning rubber and crushed metal, reminding him of Ali's death, when he wanted his memories of his wife to be only good ones.

There was no bag for Joe to pack; all he had was what he stood up in, and he looked like a vagrant.

The ward sister popped her head around the door again to tell him that Phil would be at the hospital within the hour.

True to his word, Phil walked into the ward forty minutes after he'd received the call. Joe was waiting; his discharge letter, pain medication and Alison's medical death certificate, clutched to his chest. Phil's expression reflected his sadness.

'Joe, I don't know what to say! We couldn't believe it, and I'm so very sorry, Alison was the best ... it seems so bloody unfair.'

Joe was to hear similar sentiments over the weeks to come, but he knew Phil was sincere.

'Come on, let's get you home.' Phil helped Joe to his feet and, conforming to hospital policy, steered him into a wheelchair and pushed him to the main exit. His car was parked in a pick-up zone nearby and as he settled Joe into the passenger seat he said, 'Helen says you'd be very welcome to join us for a meal later, it's going to be a bit difficult for you with that arm in a sling.'

'Thanks, Phil, I appreciate the offer but for today I think I'd just like to be at home. Another time maybe? How's Liffey? Has she been behaving for you?'

'Oh yes, she's no trouble, never is. We've been thinking about that too and we'll walk her for you until you're up to it yourself. Helen's the early bird, so she'll take her each morning and I'll take her at night.'

'That's so kind of you both and I'll happily accept your offer. I don't think I'll be up to much more than letting her in the garden for a while, but I wouldn't like her to miss her exercise.'

'Good, that's settled then. And it goes without saying that if there's anything at all we can do for you, just say the word.'

'Thanks, that means a lot, and I might just have to take you up on it too. I'll have to begin to sort out all of Ali's affairs and to be honest it scares the hell out of me!' Joe was close to tears but didn't want to break down in front of his friend.

'Well, we mean it, anything at all, mate.'

Within twenty minutes they were pulling up in front of Joe's house. Phil ran round the car and opened the door, then, taking the keys from Joe's hand, walked ahead to open the front door. He would never know what that little gesture meant to his neighbour. Joe had been dreading going into an empty house, knowing how cold and unwelcoming it would feel without Alison there waiting for him.

Almost as soon as they were inside, Helen appeared with Liffey who almost knocked her master down in her enthusiasm at seeing him. Joe sat on the sofa and stroked his dog with his good hand, trying to contain her excitement lest she knocked his injured arm. Helen, who would normally have hugged her neighbour, squeezed his hand gently,

'I'm so sorry, Joe, really I am. We'll miss Alison terribly; she was such a lovely person.' There were tears in her eyes and Joe had to swallow hard to stop himself from breaking down and sobbing openly.

'Thanks, Helen, and for having Liffey, I knew she'd be fine with you.'

'Any time, and I mean that. Not just having Liffey, who's a delight to look after, but if there's anything you need, we're here for you. Now, would you like to come and eat with us later? It's just a casserole but you're very welcome?'

'If you don't mind I'm really quite tired. I think I'll just have a quiet evening and get an early night. The doctor said I needed as much rest as I can get, although tomorrow I'll have to start making arrangements...' His voice trailed off as he thought of the bureaucracy he had to deal with.

'Ah, well,' Phil interrupted, 'I hope you don't think it presumptuous of me but I've taken a day off work tomorrow to be at your disposal. We know you have no family to speak of, so I thought perhaps I could run you about a bit, you know, the bank or wherever?'

'Oh, Phil, that is so good of you and I don't mind at all, I'm really grateful. I was awake most of last night trying to think of what I had to do, so I really would appreciate your support. I can't arrange the funeral yet though, until after the inquest but I need to get an interim death certificate from the coroner's office. Other than that I'm unsure of what else I can do.'

'Phil's auntie died last year and he was executor of her estate, so he has some idea of what needs to be done,' Helen added.

Joe's eyes started to fill up again. 'Thank you both, you've already made things so much easier for me.'

'No problem. Look I'll put the kettle on and make you a cup of tea and then we'll leave you in peace. Phil will come back at about six to walk Liffey and I'll send a bit of that casserole round, just in case you're hungry.'

Helen was only a couple of minutes and then they left Joe with a mug of hot tea, his dog by his side and instructions to call on them if he needed any help. His neighbours were exceptional people and had already stepped up to the mark, proving to be so thoughtful.

It was 3pm. Liffey settled down beside Joe on the sofa while he sipped his tea. The house felt different, empty, and hollow. Alison's presence, looking out for her husband's comfort, keeping the conversation bright and generally making their house a home, would never be felt again, leaving an almost tangible void. She was gone forever and it was going to be almost impossible to adjust.

Joe wondered if he could do it, or even if he wanted to do it. Liffey snuggled closer to him; she would be a comfort, although she would soon begin to wonder where Alison was and he knew that she too would grieve. He dropped his head into Liffey's warm fur and wept bitterly, letting all his emotions out, while his dog stayed close beside him, sensing his need of her.

CHAPTER 6

A week in hospital seemed like an eternity to Hannah. Each day dragged by with nothing to look forward to other than visits from her family and, if she was honest, even they were something of a strain.

The idea of going home simultaneously delighted and terrified her; at least in hospital help and support were on hand, embarrassing though it often was, but the thought of having to ask Mike or Mel to help her onto the toilet was awful. She hadn't yet had a proper shower, but would require help with that too, as well as dressing and all the other things she took for granted. Each little task proved to be exhausting and, on top of that, a physiotherapist came to see her each day, encouraging Hannah to exercise her good leg, as well as what was left of her right leg, at least three times a day.

'It's important to keep the muscles supple,' the physio explained. 'When you're fitted with a prosthetic leg you'll need to be able to move your thigh as normal, so we can't let the muscles atrophy; it'll cause problems later on.'

The physiotherapist was obviously good at her job and Hannah liked her. Always ready to answer questions as well as she was able, she seemed to understand the emotional side of the injury as well as the physical.

The first time the dressing was changed and Hannah saw the full extent of her loss, she was horrified and felt quite nauseous. The angry wound was like nothing she'd ever seen before and was made all the more shocking because the swollen, ugly mass of flesh she was confronted with was her own body.

After the nurse re-dressed the leg and Hannah was once more alone, she'd cried softly for almost an hour, turning towards the wall so the other patients in the room wouldn't see. Even now the shock remained, but it was easing. One of the nurses explained that what she was experiencing was a process of grieving; she'd lost a vital part of her body and needed time to mourn, to come to terms with it. Understanding this made things a little easier and Hannah didn't feel so selfish when she was suddenly struck by a bout of 'feeling sorry for herself'. She did, however, need to work through these emotions and often experienced anger, as well as sadness and loss, yet Hannah tried her best not to show how raw these feelings were, particularly to her family. When they visited, as they did regularly, she appeared cheerful, but it was an act — she hadn't yet reached the stage of feeling 'lucky', like many considered she was, to still be alive.

From various sources, Hannah gradually pieced together some of the facts about the accident, which her brain seemed to have blanked out completely. When the police first came to interview her, she felt completely useless and could tell them nothing at all about that day.

It seemed that her car had been the first to lose control on the ice and apparently skidded down the slip road, spun at an angle of 180 degrees and hit the rear of an articulated lorry on the motorway. Hannah travelled that road daily and knew she wouldn't have been speeding, especially in such awful weather conditions. The gradient on the slip road was, however, fairly steep, and the police said that even though the cars on the motorway were not speeding either, it was the domino effect of the collision which made the consequences so devastating.

In addition, when the lorry driver became aware of what was happening, he braked suddenly — a natural reaction, but one which caused his vehicle to skid towards Hannah's car and exacerbate the impact with it. Apparently the car which hit hers first held two passengers and one of them, a woman, died at the scene. Another woman and a teenage boy had also been killed as their vehicles lost control and slammed into the mangled wreckage, completely at the mercy of the ice on the roads.

It was still troubling to Hannah that she couldn't remember anything at all. The doctors said her recollections may yet come back, but worrying about it could have the opposite effect. Still, however, the niggling doubt in Hannah's mind was whether or not she could have done something to prevent the accident, or worse still, could she have done something which made her responsible for the catastrophic event?

The swelling on Hannah's leg went down considerably during her stay in hospital. It still looked grotesque, yet she felt compelled to look each time the dressing was changed. The drain had been removed and the doctor seemed pleased with the way it was healing. One thing she did find difficult, however, was hearing her leg referred to as a 'stump'. She knew it was only a word, but such an ugly word, and yet there seemed no alternative, no sanitised medical term which would make the reality more acceptable. The physio referred to her stump when she talked about how the prosthetic leg would fit, and the doctors referred to her stump when they discussed how the wound was healing. It was just something she'd have to get used to, but she determinedly avoided using the word herself, instead saying 'bad leg' when it was necessary to refer to it.

After a week, Hannah was coping with much milder painkillers, generally only paracetamol with occasional ibuprofen. One thing she did learn was that the phenomenon of 'phantom pains' was a very real and distressing fact. At times she couldn't sleep because of the 'pain' in her missing limb, or occasionally an itch, which was equally as bad. As she tossed and turned at night she grabbed at the empty space where her leg should have been, exasperated at the irrational, but very real, sensation.

After the first few days, physio was no longer conducted on her bed and Hannah was wheeled to the gym to use the parallel bars in order to help her stand, but was still required to exercise on her own in the ward, as well as the gym sessions. Crutches were introduced, but it was obviously going to take time to master using them as she was afraid of falling and damaging her bad leg, even though there was always someone close by to help if she toppled.

Going to the gym was, at least, a change of scenery, and she met other amputees who were at different stages of recovery to herself and with whom she could compare notes, and even, amazingly, have a laugh. One man who attended as an outpatient and had already been fitted with a prosthetic leg told her how he'd fallen in the bathroom.

'When I got out of the bath and was sitting on the edge to get dried, I simply forgot that I only had one leg and, silly sod that I am, set off on the missing leg and ended up flat on my face!' He was laughing about it and Hannah found herself joining in. The physio said that most patients did that at least once. Perhaps she too would one day see the funny side of losing her leg.

One of the most difficult things for Hannah to accept was the reaction of her children. Sam was very quiet during their visits, still unsure of what to say to his mother, which was to be expected for a seventeen-year-old boy. Mel was almost too gushing, probably trying to compensate for her brother's silence by filling the void with endless chatter. Mike's reaction was somewhere in between. When the children were there he made the effort to talk but when there was just the two of them, he lapsed into an almost moody silence; it was as if neither of them could think of anything to say.

'The physio said I should be able to manage the stairs on my bottom,' Hannah told him, 'and using crutches and a wheelchair in the house shouldn't be too much of a problem.'

It was a disappointment to learn that it would be several weeks before she could be fitted with a prosthetic leg; in her ignorance of such matters Hannah had assumed it would simply be a process of getting one to fit, perhaps even before she left the hospital. She'd soon learned that it was a much more complicated process and measurements couldn't be taken until her leg had reduced to its normal size.

Her husband simply nodded, which didn't make things any easier for her. She wished he'd be more positive; say how much he was missing her or something, and encourage her in the little achievements she'd already made. He gave the distinct impression that he was dreading Hannah leaving the hospital, which worried her every bit as much as the practical issues she would have to cope with.

On the morning of day eleven (Hannah had been counting religiously), the doctor said she could go home the following day, and her care would be transferred to a district nurse who would call at their home each day. Mixed feelings flooded her mind. On the positive side, she was sure there would be more chance of rest at home; the hospital was always busy and often noisy, even at night, and she did get unbelievably tired. But what if she fell when no one was there, or the pain became unbearable?

When the family arrived later that evening Hannah told them what the doctor had said.

'That's great, Mum!' Mel seemed genuinely happy and Sam smiled broadly.

'Isn't it a bit too soon?' Mike asked.

'They wouldn't let me go if they thought I wasn't ready,' Hannah almost snapped back at him, wondering if perhaps he didn't actually want her home.

'Right.' He switched into practical mode. 'They told me at work I could take some time off when I needed it, so I'll take it from tomorrow and come to get you after lunch.'

Hannah hoped the children hadn't picked up on the cool atmosphere between their parents. For many, this kind of situation would strengthen a relationship, but for them it appeared to be working in quite the opposite way; an invisible wedge seemed to be prising them even further apart than they'd been of late.

'Well, I've made a decision, Mum.' Mel announced with a nervous smile on her face. 'I've decided not to go to university, but to stay at home to look after you instead!'

'What?' Hannah couldn't believe what she'd just heard. 'You're not serious, are you?'

'Of course I am! You're far more important than university, and maybe I can get a part time job and be around the rest of the time to look after you.'

'But I'm not going to be a complete invalid! I'll get a prosthetic leg in a few weeks' time and you won't need to look after me!' Hannah reacted rather too quickly and saw tears begin to well in her daughter's eyes. Mel's ambition in life for many years had been to train as a journalist and now she was prepared to throw it all away to care for her mother. Hannah was touched and proud, as well as horrified that she might be an obstacle to her daughter's aspirations.

'Oh, Mel love, I'm sorry. I'm really grateful for your concern but the last thing I want is for you to give up university! I love you for even thinking about it, but that's not what I want for you; it wouldn't be right.'

She reached out to her daughter and Mel fell into her mother's arms and released the tears she'd so far held back. It struck Hannah then just how badly this had affected her children. As she held her daughter, Sam shuffled closer too and put his arms around her and his sister, tears in his own eyes.

They were all grieving, grief which perhaps manifested in different ways. The children were hardly mature enough to deal with what had happened to their mother and none of them as yet knew the full implications of the accident, or what the future held. While Hannah comforted her children, Mike sat to the side, an observer, a fact which didn't go unnoticed by Hannah and only added to her worries. Maybe she didn't really want to know what the future had in store for them.

CHAPTER 7

The amber liquid swirled around the glass in his hand, the winter sunshine enhancing its translucent colour, mesmerizing Joe as he studied the whisky. *'No alcohol with the painkillers'*, the doctor had emphasised, but what was the worst that could happen? Surely it already had! Joe deliberately put the glass down on the coffee table where he could see it while he decided whether or not to drink it.

After his neighbours left the previous afternoon, Joe dragged himself wearily upstairs to remove his dirty clothes. It was such an effort that he could only manage to drag on his pyjamas rather than a fresh set of clothes; he would like to live in their comfort until he felt better, there seemed to be nothing and no one to get dressed for.

Phil returned promptly at 6pm, with a generous portion of Helen's casserole, and took Liffey for a walk as promised. Joe had been sitting in the dark so Phil closed the curtains and turned on the light, without comment. Out of politeness, Joe attempted to eat the casserole while Phil was out, but ended up putting most of it into Liffey's bowl; she would enjoy it at least.

The next morning, Helen arrived early to again walk Liffey, and when she returned made a pot of tea and toasted some bread. But now it was mid-morning, the tea and toast were cold and the whisky looked so inviting. The doorbell rang before he took the first sip and Phil called out to him.

'Are you ready, Joe?'

Ready for what? Joe wondered, but then remembered that they were going to the coroner's office and the bank.

'Not dressed yet, mate?' Phil stated the obvious as he came through the doorway. 'Do you need a hand? I'm not as pretty as those hospital nurses but I'm happy to help.'

'Yes, thanks.' Joe stood up and made his way upstairs, followed by his friend who was doing his best to pretend things were normal, and tactfully didn't mention the cold tea, or the far too early glass of whisky.

Once outside, the cold air stung Joe's face, strangely making him feel somewhat better. Having a purpose took his mind off the horror of the accident and its distressing consequences.

First stop was the coroner's office where he presented the medical certificate from the hospital and, after a reasonable wait, received an interim death certificate. Next, they moved on to the bank where Alison's accounts were frozen until probate was granted on the will.

Phil seemed to understand what needed to be done and took the lead, for which Joe was grateful. There was so much to think about when all he really wanted to do was to get back home to see his dog, and feel the weight of that glass of whisky in his hand, warm and comforting.

'We wondered if you wanted us to take you to see Alison's mother this afternoon, or is it too soon?' Phil asked.

'I suppose I should, but she's really the last person I want to see. You must think me awful, but we never really hit it off and I don't think I can face her grief as well.'

'That's fine, I understand. Let us know when you do feel up to it and we'll come with you; it might make the visit easier.'

'Thanks, another day perhaps, but I'll ring her later this afternoon, although I can't tell her a date for the funeral yet, goodness knows what she'll say to that.' It wasn't a conversation he was looking forward to.

On his return, Liffey greeted Joe with her usual enthusiasm which was so welcome in his present state of mind. He let her out into the garden and then fed her before returning to the kitchen where he picked up a slice of the cold toast and ate it, all the while looking at the glass of whisky which was exactly where he'd left it.

In his heart, Joe knew that if he gave in and drank the golden liquid, it would bring only temporary relief to his grief, so with great determination he picked up the cold tea instead and put it in the microwave to re-heat. Drinking it with the other slice of toast at least took away the light-headedness he was beginning to feel.

Joe was well aware that he needed to be sensible; Alison wouldn't want him to go to pieces and would be the first one to tell him that he must go on living. He finished the tea and toast, went back into the lounge and lay down on the sofa where he closed his eyes and soon fell into a deep sleep.

The doorbell woke him and he went to answer it, finding a young police constable standing in the porch.

'Mr Parker? I'd like to ask you some questions about the road traffic accident you were involved in recently.'

The officer seemed glad to be invited inside out of the bitter wind, which was now blowing yet more snow into drifts at the side of the road.

'I'm sorry for your loss and I know this is a difficult time for you, but I'm sure you understand that we need to move ahead quickly with our investigation.'

The young officer took out a notebook and asked Joe to describe everything he remembered.

'It's a bit of a blur really,' Joe told him. 'The weather was bloody awful, rather like today but even colder, and the rain was pelting down and almost freezing as it touched the road.

We were on the motorway and the traffic was moving steadily as we approached a junction, then suddenly a Ford Focus appeared from the slip road, spun round 180 degrees, and its rear end crashed into a lorry on the motorway.' He wracked his brains trying to think of something else to say but he couldn't remember much other than that. 'I tried to brake but the brakes couldn't grip the icy road and my car skidded too. There was no way I could avoid crashing straight into the front of her car. Is she one of those who died?'

'No, the driver of the Ford Focus is still in hospital. And what happened once you were stationary?' The constable was scribbling everything down.

'We felt something crash into us from behind but with the windscreen shattered and the air bag I couldn't see what was happening outside the car ... and my wife, she was unconscious, I was focussed on her...' For an instant Joe was back in the car, calling Alison's name with no response. His eyes became moist as he swallowed hard to prevent himself from breaking down.

'I'm sorry, Mr Parker; I know this must be distressing for you. Did you feel the impact from any other vehicles at all?'

'Yes, we seemed to be jolted several times, but I don't remember exactly how many.'

'Well, if you do think of anything else would you give me a ring?' The officer handed him a card.

'It wasn't anyone's fault, was it? I mean, it was the ice that caused the accident, surely?'

'It appears so, but as with all RTAs we have to investigate and there'll be a coroner's hearing too, when you'll probably be called as a witness. We'll keep you updated with the investigation, and thanks for your help.'

When the constable left Joe thought of so many things he'd wanted to ask, like how many cars were involved and how many people injured, but he'd have to wait, probably until the inquest. *One more thing to endure alone*, he thought.

Joe was in somewhat of a daze but could put it off no longer; he picked up the telephone and tapped in his mother-in-law's number.

'About time too!' was the angry greeting from her. 'My only daughter dies and you don't phone me until three days later!'

'Ethel, I've been in hospital myself with a broken collarbone, and she wasn't only your daughter, she was my wife.' Joe really wanted to slam the phone down but he tried to exercise a degree of patience, if only for Ali's sake.

'Well, how do you think I've felt not knowing what had happened to her, and you not answering the phone?' His mother-in-law always looked at everything from her own perspective, how it would affect her, never mind anyone else.

'I did ask the chaplain in hospital to let you know. Didn't he send a policeman round to tell you?'

'He did, and what an awful way to hear such news.' Ethel sniffed, obviously disappointed with Joe, a sentiment which was pretty much par for the course. 'So who's going to look after me now? I'm nearly out of milk — can you fetch some round?'

'Ethel, I've just told you, I have a broken collarbone. The car is off the road too, but I won't be able to drive for a few weeks anyway. One of the reasons I rang was to let you know that I can't arrange a funeral until after the coroner's inquest. I don't know how long that will be but I'll let you know as soon as I do.'

'Well, perhaps you should insist that they get on with it! It's not right, my poor girl not even getting laid to rest, who do they think they are?'

'There's nothing we can do to hurry the process and it's only right that they investigate the accident. There were two others who lost their lives that day as well as Alison — we'll just have to be patient.'

'And what do I do in the meantime?' Ethel was back to thinking of herself again.

'You'll have to ring social services and ask about getting some help; I know Alison talked to you about it before.'

'But I'll have to pay for that!'

Joe was getting annoyed; it wasn't as if the old lady couldn't afford to pay for her care, money was really no problem, except that she didn't like to spend it.

'Well, I can't see any other way for now,' he said. He ended the call quickly; if he stayed on the line much longer he'd almost certainly have said something he would later regret. Ethel was hardly reacting like a grieving mother, but for Alison's sake he would try to be civil to his mother-in-law.

CHAPTER 8

Hannah struggled from the car into the house on her crutches. She'd mastered using them in the hospital, but the corridors there were straight and smooth, while negotiating the garden gate and the crazy-paved path to her house was like walking through an obstacle course. Concentrating hard on her balance, remembering what they'd taught her in physio, she was still afraid that she might fall flat on her face.

Next door's curtains twitched, giving away the fact that Rosie was watching, another reason not to fall over. Rosie had visited the hospital on only one occasion, bringing with her a welcome bundle of luxury toiletries, magazines and Hannah's favourite chocolates. She stayed only a short time, seeing how tired her friend was, but insisted that she send a message through Mike if there was anything else she needed. Hannah was grateful for Rosie's sensitivity and looked forward to seeing her properly now that she was home.

Once inside the house, she was greeted enthusiastically by Mel and almost as keenly by Sam. It was Saturday and they were all at home together, an unusual occurrence for the Graham family.

'I'll make tea!' Mel bounded off to the kitchen to perform a task that would normally have been her mother's.

Hannah was again struck by how different life was going to be, certainly until the fitting of her prosthetic leg. She sat on the sofa with her feet up; it was important to keep her stump elevated, as well as moving her leg as much as possible. Mike sat facing her on an armchair and Sam hovered, unsure what his role should be.

'Come here.' She smiled and motioned to her son, who dutifully perched on the sofa beside her. She took his hand. 'I know it's difficult for you, love, but we will get through this, I promise!'

Sam leaned on his mother's shoulder and allowed her to hold him for a few brief moments. She could tell he was close to tears but knowing Sam he wouldn't give way easily. He sat up suddenly.

'Rosie's coming up the path.' He'd spotted their neighbour over his mother's shoulder and now pulled away from her.

'Well, she hasn't wasted any time!' Mike moaned.

'Why shouldn't she come round?'

'She's hardly given you any time to settle in, has she?'

'Rosie's my friend, Mike, and I'd like to see her. Could you open the door please?'

Mike rose to let their neighbour in with a scowl on his face, and then made an excuse about going out to get a takeaway for them to eat, leaving his wife and children wondering at his rudeness.

'How are you, Hannah?' Rosie asked, moving to carefully hug her.

Mel brought in a tray of tea and then she and Sam tactfully left the two women alone.

'If I'm absolutely honest, awful!' Hannah had tears in her eyes. 'I've been feeling sorry for myself but at the same time trying to make Mike and the kids feel better about this whole thing. It's so hard on the kids, and Mike avoids any serious conversation. I want to help them cope but it's a two-way street, surely?'

'Of course it is! And you have every right to indulge in a bloody pity party if you want to; it's been a nightmare for you and it'll take more than just a few days to adjust! Mike will come round and as for Mel and Sam, well they're young and resilient, they'll cope.'

'Mel's talking about not going to university ... but I can't let her do that. This is my problem and I don't want it to affect her future!'

'Then tell her that. Look, none of you know how this is going to impact on you as a family, it's early days yet, but there's no reason why you can't resume a normal life when your leg's healed and you get a prosthetic one, which I presume is the aim?'

'Yes it is, although I don't know how I'll manage with it.' Hannah noticed Rosie's eyes straying to where her right leg should be. In the hospital she'd seen others doing the same too when she was out of bed and sitting in a chair, an almost morbid curiosity, as if they wanted to make certain that her leg really was gone. 'It's ugly, isn't it? And such an ugly name too, a "stump". I wake up every morning thinking I'm whole ... and then I remember, I no longer have a leg, just a "stump".' Hannah bit her bottom lip, not wanting to break down.

'You're still Hannah, still the same woman, wife and mother, and my friend. Nothing can change that.' Rosie had tears in her eyes too.

'Thanks, Rosie, you're a brick.'

Rosie reached down to hug her.

'Now listen, I don't want to become a nuisance, always popping in and such like, but I want you to promise me that you'll ring if I can do anything at all, or if ever you need a shoulder to cry on, okay?'

Hannah nodded and smiled; she would like that, she'd always been able to talk to Rosie and her earthy common sense was probably exactly what she needed now. Although there was almost ten years' age difference between the two women, they'd been friends for years, opposites in many ways but always there for each other.

Rosie was the younger of the two — a fiery, opinionated woman, married to Frank, a quiet, unassuming man who adored his wife. Their relationship had often puzzled Hannah; she rarely managed to get a full sentence of conversation from Frank, whereas his wife offered an opinion on every subject, whether it was asked for or not. Still they appeared to get on well together, each doing their own thing, but utterly devoted to one another.

Rosie's long-term plan for her life was well defined and almost set in stone. It basically consisted of promotion at work by the time she was thirty, her first child at thirty-two and their second and final child, at thirty-five. Frank was apparently content to let her make such decisions, nor did he seem to mind the time she devoted to her wide circle of friends, including Hannah, for which the latter was extremely grateful, especially now. She supposed he had his football; a season ticket holder at Manchester City, Frank never missed a match, home or away and still played in a local Sunday league. Rosie often said she would never dare to ask her husband to choose between her and football, and Hannah hoped she was joking.

The sound of Mike's car in the drive prompted Rosie to say goodbye. 'Remember, any time,' she repeated as she left.

Mike carried a bundle of fish and chips under his arm and called the children downstairs to help set a tray. They ate on their knees; it was easier than attempting to get Hannah to the table. After they'd eaten, while the twins cleared away, she tried to talk to Mike.

'I'm going to have to make some effort to move around the house. If you could bring the wheelchair in from the car, perhaps I could sit in it and get from here into the kitchen and the downstairs toilet ... but I might need some help when I'm in there, is that all right?'

Mike's brow furrowed. 'Do you want me to help with that sort of thing, or Mel?'

'Well, if you don't want to...' Hannah was horrified. Did she disgust her husband so much? If he couldn't bear the thought of helping her with such a basic task, how on earth would she manage? 'It won't be forever, you know! When I'm fitted with a new leg I'll be pretty independent again.' Mike's expression was unreadable, a mixture of disgust and pity, but whether for himself or his wife, Hannah couldn't tell. 'What is it, Mike, what's wrong?'

'Oh, nothing's wrong, everything's wonderful!' His sarcasm shocked her. 'It's all this — everything — why did it have to happen?'

'How should I know? I didn't ask to lose my leg, you know, and I like it even less that you do!'

Both their voices were raised now. Hannah couldn't understand why her husband seemed so angry with her; did he somehow blame her for the accident? Mike looked at her for a moment and then grabbed his jacket.

'I'm going out!' he snapped and headed for the door.

'Yes, go on then, run away while you can be sure I can't run after you!'

As she heard the door slam Hannah regretted her last comment. She'd barely been home for two hours and they were arguing already. Perhaps she should have expected it; things hadn't been right between them for a while, but she'd ignored the whole situation, head in the sand as usual. Now it would be twice as bad with the extra pressure of her injury, but she'd at least hoped for a little compassion from her husband.

If he couldn't show her any now, what did that tell her about the state of their marriage and their long term future?

'What's going on, Mum?' Mel appeared in the doorway, looking anxious.

'Nothing for you to worry about. Your dad and I are just both a bit stressed, love, that's all. It's all going to take some getting used to, I'm afraid.'

'Dad shouldn't be shouting at you though, it's the last thing you need.'

'Please don't worry about it; it'll all blow over soon.' Hannah was trying to reassure herself as much as Mel, but Mike's attitude was worrying — was there something else going on with him, she wondered?

Hannah was exhausted, which seemed to be a permanent state of affairs at the moment, but she needed to use the toilet and there was no option other than to ask Mel for help. Her daughter was less embarrassed than she was and soon Hannah was again back on the sofa, her eyes closed, hoping Mike would be back soon with an apology, which she would gladly reciprocate. They would have to address the tension they were both feeling, but perhaps if she slept now she'd feel more able to cope when he did come home.

The next thing Hannah was aware of was the sound of the car in the drive. Mike was home. Mel and Sam were both in their rooms which would give them opportunity to talk; she was almost holding her breath as he opened the front door.

'There's a policeman just arriving,' were his first words, so any discussion would obviously have to wait until later.

The same young constable who'd interviewed Hannah in hospital stepped into the lounge.

'Hello, Mrs Graham, how are you?'

'Better for being home, thank you,' she answered nervously.

'Good, well I'm sorry to trouble you again and especially over the weekend, but it's just to find out if you've remembered anything at all about the accident yet?'

'No, I'm sorry, it's still a blank. I've been trying not to worry about it in the hope that my memory will return soon. Is there a problem?'

'Only in that you're not going to be in a position to be a witness to what happened, and your vehicle was apparently key to the whole accident. If you can't help us in any way then we'll have to rely on the evidence of the others involved, although we'd rather have the complete picture. The coroner's hearing has been set for Tuesday 20th February. You'll be getting written confirmation of the date and will be expected to attend; will that be a problem for you?' The young man looked automatically at Hannah's leg, then quickly away again, embarrassed by the lapse.

Hannah looked at Mike for an answer; she was in his hands as far as being able to get anywhere was concerned. He answered for her.

'Yes, we'll be able to attend. It seems very soon. Is that usual?' he asked.

'The coroner tries to have the inquest as soon as possible, as the, er, the families of the victims are not able to arrange the funerals until it's over.'

'Of course, how very difficult for them.' Hannah's heart went out to those grieving. Waiting for the funeral must only serve to increase their grief.

'Can you give us an idea of what will happen? It's all very new to us. Is it like a trial?' Mike asked.

'No, it's much less formal than a trial, and without a jury or anything like that. The purpose is simply to look at all the evidence and hear from the witnesses in order for the coroner to decide what caused the accident and subsequent deaths, and then to rule on his findings.'

'Have you any idea what that ruling might be?' Mike asked the question both he and Hannah were dreading hearing the answer to.

'Well, he will be looking for possible culpability; what, or possibly who, caused the accident and depending on his verdict, charges might follow.' The constable looked embarrassed to be telling them this, but his feelings weren't anything like as raw as Hannah's. She listened in silence, each one of the constable's words reverberating in her mind, fear and uncertainty growing unchecked. If only she could remember!

'So what kind of charges?' Mike pushed the young officer a little further, despite his obvious reluctance.

'At the very worst, manslaughter, or possibly causing death by reckless driving, or driving without due care and attention. Look, I wouldn't worry about this now. Everyone's agreed that the conditions were appalling and the coroner may decide on a no fault verdict. But if you do remember anything which could help us, please get in touch as soon as possible.'

The officer couldn't get out of the house quickly enough. His words offered very little in the way of comfort to Hannah, who was now quite pale, her head spinning with the implications of what she'd just heard. Wriggling uncomfortably in her seat she waited for Mike to return, wondering how he would react to the news. His words shocked her even more.

'Are you sure you don't remember anything about the accident?'

'Of course I don't — do you think I'm lying?' She was horrified that he felt he needed to ask such a question.

'No of course not ... but perhaps it's just that you don't want to remember?'

'Mike! You think I caused the accident, don't you? How could you?'

'Well, if you can't remember, how can you be sure you didn't cause it? I don't mean intentionally, of course, but perhaps you tried to speed up a little to get onto the motorway, you know you're always last minute for work, always in a hurry?'

'But I wouldn't do that! I've never taken risks while driving and you know it.' She looked at her husband with wide, disbelieving eyes. 'You don't really think I could be charged with anything, do you?'

Hannah was really scared now. Remembering suddenly took on a whole new importance, and her head ached with the fear that she might somehow be to blame for the accident, to have had a hand in the deaths of three innocent people! It was an unbearable thought and tears rolled down her face as her mind raced ahead to the worst possible scenario she could think of — a charge for manslaughter! Could things possibly get any worse?

CHAPTER 9

Liffey barked as the letters plopped through the letterbox and landed on the doormat. Joe collected them, sorting them into two piles, one for shredding and the other to be opened. Mostly they were the usual bills and circulars, but one envelope was unfamiliar and looked somewhat official, so he opened it first.

Staring at the page, he first noticed the words 'Coroner's Inquest' and quickly scanning the page, the date, 20th February 2018. It was another stage in the process and one he'd be glad to get over, not least because then he would be able to arrange Alison's funeral.

Joe had never before considered what was associated with a death, and ironically it was almost certainly the worst possible time to absorb and understand everything which needed to be done. Having his arm in a sling and the constant pain of his injury didn't help either; it was a surprise to him how difficult it was to manage even the simplest of tasks with one arm incapacitated. He propped the letter on the mantel shelf behind the clock and sighed; whatever the coroner's findings would be, they wouldn't bring Alison back.

Joe was due at the hospital for an X-ray. If his bones were not healing, he faced the prospect of surgery to have a metal plate fitted, an unpleasant thought which had gone some way to ensuring he was looking after himself and not attempting to use his injured arm. Phil again volunteered a lift; he and Helen were a true godsend and Joe didn't know how he'd have coped without their practical help and support.

As Phil drove through the early morning traffic, Joe found himself flinching each time another car approached — unnecessarily so, as Phil was an excellent driver. He supposed it was a natural reaction to having been in a serious accident and only hoped it wouldn't affect his confidence when he was able to get back behind the wheel himself. At one point Joe suddenly braced himself, convinced they were going to collide with another car.

'You all right, mate?' Phil asked.

'Yes, sorry, I'm a bit of a nervous passenger these days.'

Phil nodded in understanding.

The early appointment ensured that Joe didn't have long to wait, so they went first to the X-ray department and then to the waiting room. He was called in after only fifteen minutes and received the good news that the X-ray showed that the bones were knitting together well and the doctor seemed pleased with his progress.

'We'll do another X-ray in two weeks' time and if things are still improving you can start physio and begin to use the arm again. Keep resting it until then and if it's still looking good I think we can forget about surgery.'

The doctor smiled, delighted to be offering good news. It was such a relief to Joe, the last thing he wanted was for his injury to need further treatment; his caution over the last couple of weeks seemed to have paid off. After the appointment he insisted on buying Phil a coffee in the hospital cafe, it was the least he could do to repay his friend.

'I got a letter about the inquest this morning, it's on the 20th of this month,' he told Phil.

'Do you want me to come with you, or is it just for family?'

'If you can, that would be great. I don't have much in the way of family really — only a brother who I haven't had contact with for years and the mother-in-law from hell. Doesn't that just describe what a sad life I have?'

'Ah, but you have friends.' Phil grinned.

'That I have, and you've proved to be the best, Phil. I'm so grateful to you and Helen; I really don't know how I'd have coped without you both.'

'We've done no more than anyone else would do. We were both very fond of Alison and we miss her too, I still can't believe what happened sometimes and I actually think you're coping remarkably well. If it was Helen who'd gone, I'd be a complete wreck.'

'Most of the time I function on auto-pilot. Night times are the worst, it's almost unbearable and I don't sleep too well these days. I dread those small hours of the morning, but daylight comes eventually and I've got Liffey to keep going for. Sounds silly, doesn't it, she's just a dog, but sometimes I think she understands what I'm going through.'

'Of course she does! Dogs are very sensitive creatures and she'll pick up on your feelings. And she must miss Alison too.'

'Yes, I think she does.'

They were silent for a few moments and then Phil asked when Joe would be considering starting work again.

'I'd actually like to get back as soon as possible but with this collarbone, it's not an option yet. Perhaps after the inquest and the next visit here? I'll discuss it with the doctor then, see what he thinks.'

'It might be good to focus on something else and I know you enjoy your work. They seem to have been quite flexible with you too,' Phil remarked.

'Yes, they have. One of the directors rang me almost as soon as I got home from the hospital and told me to take as much time as I needed. They sent a lovely bouquet of flowers too;

Ali would have loved them...' Joe's voice was fractured and he was in danger of losing it, a definite no-no in public! He sniffed, raised his eyes and forced himself to smile. 'You're right, it will do me good to get back to work, some sort of routine and all that.'

'Helen and I were talking about it too and we want you to know that we'll be happy to keep on helping with Liffey's care. We'll see to her during the day, or at least Helen will when I'm at work, in fact she can come to us any time you're not at home if you like. You know we love to have her — it could be a kind of dog-share?'

Joe hadn't even considered such practicalities, but Liffey, although happy to be left alone sometimes, was used to Ali being around most days, it wouldn't be fair to leave her alone all day and every day.

'That's so kind of you and perfect for Liffey. I've not given much thought to the logistics of going back to work, apart from wondering when I'll be able to drive again. It's going to take some getting used to not having Ali around to think of all these things for me,' he replied pensively.

Once Joe was back at home, and after an enthusiastic welcome from his dog, he sat down, rubbing Liffey's ears thoughtfully as he considered his future. The house was still full of Alison; he hadn't even begun to think about sorting out her possessions, although he knew he'd have to be practical at some point.

He gave Liffey her dinner and then ventured upstairs, turning automatically towards the spare bedroom, which his wife had used as her sewing room. He'd purposely not entered this room since the accident and almost as soon as he opened the door, he wished he hadn't. It was a good sized, bright room, full of natural light from windows on two elevations, but the room was saturated with Alison's presence, as if she'd left it only a moment ago, to return at any moment. Her sewing machine, perched on the work table, still held fabric under the presser foot, where she'd left it the night before she died; too tired to put it away and assuming she'd pick up her task the following evening. Joe touched the fabric — cushion covers, that was her latest project, a change from the endless soft toys she loved to make to sell at fundraising events for the hospice.

The faint smell of one of Alison's scented candles lingered in the air. She knew he disliked them, so used them only in her own space; sweet-pea, mimosa, lilac and tea rose, being her favourite fragrances. On the shelves were her most loved books; all eight of the Brontë sisters' novels, the complete works of Jane Austen and Daphne du Maurier, together with some of her favourite contemporary authors, such as Kate Morton and Victoria Hislop.

Photographs decorated almost the whole of one wall, mostly pictures of Liffey, and others of the wonderful holidays they'd shared together. The sudden ache in his heart made him realise how much he missed his wife and how she would love to have had children's photographs in her room ... images of their children ... who had never been born.

Joe was suddenly aware of his dog in the room with him, sniffing in every corner and giving a little whine, not comprehending the finality of death, but then did he? Man and dog sat together in that small room, surrounded by memories and Alison's simple treasures, until dusk wrapped itself around them and Liffey again whined, this time for something as basic as a need to go into the garden.

CHAPTER 10

February 20th was a wild, blustery morning. Hannah hadn't slept the night before; she hadn't really slept well since the visit from the police constable signalled the possibility of charges in relation to the accident. Until then it wasn't something she'd even considered, assuming it was the atrocious weather conditions which were to blame, but now her thinking had shifted and the possibility of being somehow culpable herself haunted her waking hours and prevented any restful sleep.

Mike didn't want to talk about it, arguing that it was stupid to anticipate something which might never happen. As she hadn't told the children of her fears, it was almost impossible to get Mike alone to talk about anything serious, a situation which Hannah found increasingly frustrating. There was only Rosie to whom she could confide. Rosie, who felt angry on her behalf at the very suggestion that she had caused the accident, and who might possibly stand up and give the coroner a piece of her unique wisdom, if he should reach the conclusion that she was in any way to blame. She was grateful for her friend's loyal and fierce support and wished Mike was equally as protective.

Hannah asked Mel and Sam not to attend the inquest, afraid of what they might hear. The ban didn't go down well and eventually she'd pleaded with them not to go, getting so upset that they felt obliged to agree.

With echoes of the constable's words, '*manslaughter*' and '*driving without due care and attention*' playing on a loop through her mind, Hannah set off with Mike to discover her fate. A wheelchair was now her usual aid to mobility for any distance, as crutches still proved to be clumsy, unless on even ground.

She'd had the first measurements taken for a prosthetic leg to be made and dearly hoped she would be upright and walking again soon.

Still embarrassed at the missing limb, Hannah chose to cover herself with a rug whenever she was going out; something Mike was quick to assist with when he lifted her from the car. She was glad of its warmth today too, as she shivered with the cold, and fraught nerves. If she'd still had two legs Hannah didn't think they would have held her up that morning; she was trembling and felt sick to the stomach, anticipating the worst possible outcome.

The coroner's court was in a wing of the town hall which they entered through the disabled entrance at the side of the impressive Victorian building. The entrance hall they found themselves in was vast, its high ceiling throwing back loud echoes of visitors' shoes, or in Hannah's case, the squeaking of wheels. Rosie met them inside; she'd taken a couple of hours off work to attend, and squeezed her friend's hand in greeting, comfort which Hannah badly needed. An usher showed them the way, holding doors open for Mike to circumnavigate the obstacles of the old building.

As they entered the room, which was smaller and more comfortable than Hannah expected, people turned to look at her, some smiling weakly, sympathetically even, and others turning away, either with apathy or embarrassment. Mostly their faces were grim, red eyes from weeping or not sleeping, she couldn't tell, but Hannah felt the weight of each person's sorrow. Mike sat beside her, his face reflecting the solemnity of everyone else, while Rosie sat on his other side and leaned over to whisper encouragement.

'Well, it's not going to be easy but it'll soon be over!' She smiled, hopefully.

Or will it just be beginning? Hannah thought and blinked back the tears forming in her eyes.

The first surprise was when the coroner introduced herself as a doctor; Hannah expected a judge, or perhaps a magistrate. Dr Eloise Phillips sat at a small table with several files in front of her and began by acknowledging the tragedy of the accident and offering her condolences. She moved swiftly on to stating the purpose of the hearing, which was to rule on the cause of death of the three people who died as a result of the incident. She outlined the procedure, what was expected of each witness and, the second surprise for Hannah, the fact that anyone in the assembly could ask questions.

The first witness to be called was the police traffic officer who had been first to arrive on the scene. He looked to Hannah to be not much older than Sam as he stood nervously at a small podium next to the coroner's table and spoke from his notes. He informed the gathering that there had been eleven vehicles involved in the accident, one of the worst he'd personally ever had to deal with. This was the first of many facts the assembled group would hear, most of them distressing, and it wasn't long before quiet sobs could be heard throughout the room. Hannah's own face was wet with silent tears as she listened to the full horrors of the event of which she still had no recollection whatsoever.

It was obvious that the inquest would take several hours and due to the distressing nature of much of the evidence, the coroner halted the proceedings frequently for short breaks. Some left the room to compose themselves during these breaks, while others stayed in their seats and whispered together with grim faces.

'I don't think I can do this.' A distraught Hannah turned to Mike.

'You don't have a choice, but your evidence will be short, seeing as how you can't remember anything.' When he referred to her memory loss, Mike still sounded as if he didn't fully believe her and his attitude was almost one of annoyance.

'You'll be fine, and the coroner's obviously sympathetic.' Rosie was more encouraging but Hannah still felt that if she could walk she might just get up and flee from the room.

Some of the hardest evidence to listen to was from those who had lost loved ones in the accident. The father of the teenage boy who died had been driving him to the orthodontist, and tears rolled down his cheeks as he relived the horror of that morning. The man whose wife died also gave evidence and Hannah thought there was something familiar about his face. He described how his Range Rover had crashed into her car, the brakes impotent on the ice. His evidence was perhaps the most compelling of all and also the most comforting to Hannah. When the coroner asked his opinion of the speed her Ford Focus was travelling at the time, his reply was probably the most crucial of all the witness statements.

'It can't have been more than ten miles an hour, if that. She was on the slip road; it was the ice on the roads which caused the accident, not speeding. The poor woman didn't stand a chance when her car skidded, the conditions were atrocious and she probably hit black ice.'

After hearing all the other evidence, some of which was conflicting, this man's seemed the most powerful. His had been the second vehicle to collide and his wife was killed instantly, yet he spoke fairly and with compassion for Hannah's helplessness, which went a long way to relieving some of the anxiety she'd been feeling.

When she was eventually called to give evidence, Mike pushed her to the podium and left the chair at its side. The coroner asked her to give her name and address and to confirm her car make and registration number. Hannah trembled as she answered, her voice barely a whisper but the coroner was sympathetic and went on to ask if she had any recollection of the accident at all. The negative answer was obviously expected and Dr Phillips thanked Hannah for attending and said she could return to her seat. Rosie offered a huge 'told you so' smile as Mike pushed her back and all three felt an enormous sense of relief that this had been all which was required of her.

The hearing broke late for lunch with all the evidence having been presented and only a few questions asked by individuals in the gathering, which Dr Phillips, or the police officer, answered capably and to the apparent satisfaction of the enquirers. The coroner told them that she would sum up and present her findings when they returned from lunch.

It seemed that the main business of the day was finished. Rosie and Mike spent the lunch break offering each other reassurance that the inquest went much better than they'd hoped, but Hannah still had a sickening knot of uneasiness in the pit of her stomach. She desperately needed to hear the coroner saying categorically that she had not been at fault.

Her wish was granted after the lunch break. Dr Phillips again offered condolences to those who'd lost loved ones and then went on to announce that after consultation with the police, she was satisfied that the incident was a no-fault accident and therefore the fatalities, Marjorie Simpson, Alison Jane Parker and Timothy Gary Jones, would be recorded as accidental deaths.

As a low murmur of voices swept around the room the coroner thanked everyone for giving their time in attending and stood to leave the room. Mike was the next one to jump up, steering Hannah to the door they had entered by, as if in a hurry to get out, but his wife wasn't complaining. She felt emotionally drained and totally exhausted by the whole experience and although she would have liked to thank the man who had spoken on her behalf, she was happy to leave.

Rosie was dashing back to work, having been away much longer than anticipated.

'I'll pop in to see how you are this evening,' she told Hannah. 'I'm so glad they've seen reason!'

Hannah smiled her thanks and allowed Mike to lift her into the car. He hadn't as yet offered any opinion and his expression was unreadable.

'What do you think, Mike?' she asked him.

'Yes, a good result — it seems to have been just an unfortunate accident.'

His reply wasn't what she'd hoped to hear and lacked something, although she didn't quite know what; conviction perhaps?

The journey home passed mostly in silence and, once inside, Hannah asked Mike to help her upstairs to bed, where she pulled the quilt up to her chin and fell into a deep, dreamless sleep.

CHAPTER 11

The inquest was torture for Alan and Cassie Jones. Alan sat bolt upright beside his wife, holding her hand but lost in his own thoughts and unable to give her the comfort she craved. Cassie's parents sat on her other side and Alan's widowed mother beside him. Not only were the family forced to once again confront their own grief and relive the accident, but they were also unwilling witnesses to the grief and pain of the others who had been involved too.

Many lives were brutally affected that day; the ice had been a savage instrument of destruction to so many. One man had lost his wife, who was also a mother of four and a grandmother. Another man also lost his wife and seemed alone and totally bereft, even though outwardly he appeared composed, his face was ashen, his eyes dull and lifeless, empty. The woman in the wheelchair, they learned, had lost her leg and still had no memory of the accident itself.

Cassie felt an overwhelming empathy for all of the victims and prayed silently that out of something so brutal and far-reaching, lessons might be learned and compassion would somehow blossom out of such incomprehensible tragedy.

Timothy had taught them so much in his short life. He loved unconditionally, he cared for the feelings of other people, and he had an all-consuming passion for animals. He'd grown up fascinated by his father's work and attended clinic with his dad whenever he was allowed. From the age of seven, he began to 'collect' animals of his own which he cared for on the family's small farm.

Timothy had grown up with dogs and cats but wanted more, so when he found an injured owl, he nursed it back to health under his father's guidance. The chickens came next and then an orphaned pygmy goat, called George, all extra work for Cassie but she was amazed at how hard Timothy was prepared to work, even at such a young age. The farm outbuildings became home to any animals that needed one, and over the years even Timothy lost count of the number and variety of animals they had fostered.

Cassie and Alan Jones wanted to do something significant to honour the memory of their son, something he would have loved and which would make him proud. Now that the inquest was over, they could start thinking about what it was Timmy would have wanted.

CHAPTER 12

To have no memory of the accident; was that a blessing or a curse, Joe wondered when he arrived home from the coroner's inquest. It had been a gruelling day, but not only for him. The father of Timothy Jones looked like a broken man, and Hannah Graham seemed to be in another world, probably still in shock at the loss of her leg.

Joe was content with the verdict, even if Ethel was not. As he helped his mother-in-law into a taxi after the hearing, she was still grumbling, muttering that someone should be held accountable for the death of her daughter. The black look she gave him suggested she was thinking that he was that 'someone', making him instinctively want to counter her argument by suggesting that if Ethel herself had not been so insistent that her daughter attend her that day, Alison would not have been with him in the car.

But you could argue the toss about it all day; *if* the motorway had been closed, *if* the slip road had been gritted, *if* the Ford Focus had set off two minutes later, *if* he hadn't had toast for breakfast... 'If' was such a sad, lonely word, and a rather senseless one too. No one could have foreseen what would happen that morning or they would all have stayed safely at home.

Joe's next hurdle was to get through the funeral, and he'd made an appointment with the undertaker for the following morning. Having to wait until after the inquest to arrange Alison's funeral only added to his distress — it was an event which was permanently on his mind, one he dreaded as the final goodbye to his beloved wife. A few well-meaning people suggested that he would feel better after the funeral and that life would return to some semblance of normality, but was that what he really wanted? It would be a relief to get rid of the terrible pain he felt at his loss, but not at the expense of forgetting his wife — he would never want to do that!

Joe spoke to the undertaker and a date was fixed for ten days' time. Joe was happy to leave the arrangement of most of the details to him; it was difficult enough thinking about your wife in a coffin without deciding exactly what it was to look like. Perhaps he'd pay more in the end, but he agreed to the undertaker arranging the flowers, the obituary in the paper and other little details which were too painful for him to even think about.

Alison's funeral was every bit as grim as Joe expected it to be. The weather at least had improved, with rising temperatures melting the snow almost as swiftly as it had arrived, but still two weeks too late to spare Alison's life. The good turnout was something of a surprise to him, although it shouldn't have been; his wife was much loved by everyone she came into contact with. Neighbours and friends mingled with a few distant relatives, mainly Alison's cousins, whom he hardly knew. Many of the faces he didn't even recognise; staff from the local hospice where she volunteered each week, and a group from Ali's Pilates class all shook Joe's hand, offering the usual platitudes. He went through the motions, his own personal sorrow clamped down somewhere deep inside of him, as he thanked people for coming, playing the host for as long as he must.

Alison's mother clung to his arm throughout the service and committal, her grief well aired for all to see. If it hadn't been for his neighbour, Helen, taking her from him when they arrived at the hotel for refreshments afterwards, Joe would probably have told her to shut up, or worse.

To Joe's surprise, his brother David made the journey to the funeral with his wife, Pam, a woman Joe had only met on a handful of occasions and never quite taken to. They were staying at a Travelodge nearby for a couple of days and expressed a desire to see Joe the next day, 'to catch up', they said. He really could have done without the bother, but they'd made the effort to come so he felt obliged to invite them round to the house the following morning.

The hotel provided a pretty standard finger buffet — sandwiches with the crusts cut off, sausage rolls, quiche, pork pies and assorted nuts and crisps. Joe watched as people talked and laughed as at any other social occasion and he felt remote, like an outsider, looking in on something which didn't concern him at all. It seemed as if his head would burst from the cocktail of emotions he felt; sorrow, regret, anger and frustration, but there was nothing he could do; his wife was gone and he was left behind to carry on alone.

Joe longed for the hands on the clock to move more swiftly so that he could get home to be alone, just him and his dog. But the time ticked by unhurriedly, not caring what he wanted. He couldn't, didn't want to, believe that these people were assembled because Alison was dead; his beautiful Ali who no longer walked, breathed and laughed on this earth. How he wished he had died with her — he wanted no part of a world without her, but he must speak to these people and listen to their anecdotes of times spent with his wife. He continued to play the part. You can still exist without living, can't you?

The time did pass, although much slower than Joe wished, and at last he found himself home, driven by Phil and Helen who then kindly took Ethel home too. He'd had a whisky and a pint at the hotel and was now tired, so after letting Liffey out into the garden, he lay down on the sofa, careful not to jar his arm, and fell into a deep sleep.

The sound of the doorbell broke into his rest. It had turned dark outside whilst he slept and Phil stood on the doorstep waiting to take Liffey out for her evening walk.

'Bearing up, mate?' he asked.

'Yes, glad it's all over to be honest, and you've been brilliant, Phil. Thank you for looking after Ethel. I really couldn't take her complaints today.'

'No problem. Helen was the one to see to her mostly, I was just the driver. It was good that your brother came. I managed to have a brief word with him. Will he be staying on at all?' Phil asked.

'Apparently, yes, they've booked in at the Travelodge and are coming round tomorrow. I can't say we've ever been close and I'm rather surprised that they came, actually.'

'Family can surprise you sometimes, and the company might just be what you need.'

Phil meant well but Joe really wasn't looking forward to seeing David and Pam — it was just something else he'd have to make an effort for.

When Phil left, Joe made a token gesture at tidying up, difficult with only one arm, and then watched a mindless programme on television, before deciding on an early night.

The tears came again in the darkness of his bedroom, the bed so vast and empty without Ali. Was it better to think about her, or to try not to? Joe really didn't know. Liffey, sensing his distress, jumped up on the bed beside him and licked his arm. He spoke to her, confiding how much he missed Alison and how he dreaded each new day without her. Liffey nuzzled into his side, understanding that all was not well, and eventually they both slept.

David and Pam arrived on the doorstep at 10am, wide smiles on their faces as they marched into the lounge.

'How are you today, Joe? It's such a lovely morning after all that snow,' David said. His question and apparent upbeat mood was so totally incongruent to the whole situation that it sparked anger in Joe, who replied sharply.

'How do you think I bloody feel? I buried my wife yesterday!'

Pam's mouth dropped open and David countered, 'There's no need to snap. I was only trying to cheer you up.'

'Sorry, but please don't expect me to be "cheered up" so easily. I just can't do it.' Joe sat down and his visitors followed suit. 'It's too soon, David, and yesterday was a nightmare. I feel absolutely washed out today.'

'Right, well, how about a cup of tea and we can have a chat then?'

Joe wished his brother would go away and take his grinning wife with him, but he dutifully rose and went into the kitchen to make tea. Pam followed after him a minute or two later, asking if she could help, although by the way she was gazing around, Joe thought she was simply keen to see more of the house.

'Yes please, if you could carry the tray for me?' With his sling it was obvious he couldn't perform even such a simple task.

'Oh, yes of course!' Pam picked up the tray and carried it through to the lounge where she placed it on the glass coffee table. David meanwhile, had occupied himself by looking at the group of photographs which Ali had arranged on an occasional table in the window. They were mainly of the two of them in various holiday destinations, the usual tourist backgrounds.

'Seems you had some pretty good holidays?' David remarked, a brittle note of envy in his voice.

'Yes.' Joe could think of nothing else to say. Was his brother trying to emphasise the fact that there would be no more holidays with Alison?

'Well, that's the advantage of not having any kids, I suppose. Mind you, even without them we could never afford anything other than a caravan at Margate.' He chuckled as if he'd made a hilarious joke.

Advantage! Joe could have screamed at his brother. He'd almost forgotten how insensitive David could be ... and how jealous he always was of their lifestyle. As he handed out tea and biscuits he bit his tongue to stop himself from being rude and desperately hoped they wouldn't stay long.

'So will you be selling this place now?' Pam asked bluntly. 'It's far too big for one, surely?' She was gazing round the room as if appraising its value. 'How many bedrooms is it — three or four?'

'I've no plans for doing any such thing. This is where I feel closest to Ali, all my memories are here.'

'Yes, but you have to be sensible and think of the future,' David chipped in.

'Good grief, man, the funeral was only yesterday! I'm only just getting by one day at a time, never mind the future!'

'But you must have thought about it, and there'll be a nice hefty insurance payment due, no doubt. You'll be able to get a nice little bungalow somewhere, or perhaps one of those new executive apartments, they're perfect for single people.'

Joe's brother amazed him. 'I haven't thought about anything of the sort — and why the sudden interest, David? Why turn up after never even returning our Christmas cards for the past few years? What is it you want?'

'We don't want anything! We're family and we want to comfort you, to help if we can. Alison was a lovely woman ... but she's gone now and you've got to be practical.'

'Perhaps we are family, David, but you obviously don't know me, so why should you think you can advise me now?' Joe was furious with his insensitive, meddling brother and was almost on the point of asking him to leave when David saved him the trouble and stood up.

'There's really no need to be so rude. I can see we've caught you on a bad day so we'll go now and give you a little space. I'll be in touch when you've had time to get used to your new situation. Goodbye, Joe.' And with that the pair left their half-drunk cups of tea and let themselves out of the front door.

Joe was both angry and bemused. It was obvious that his brother felt no real concern for him. Even as children they were never close. He remembered David as a greedy, sly boy who liked nothing more than to get him into trouble with their parents, a more than frequent occurrence. Why then did he suddenly decide to play the concerned elder brother now, unless of course there was something in it for himself?

CHAPTER 13

As the weeks passed, Hannah slowly began to accept her 'stump', although the word itself still didn't sit well with her and she avoided using it. Her choice of clothing was now invariably trousers and even at home she kept her legs covered up. Mike seemed to prefer her to do so too, and on the odd occasion he'd walked into the bathroom and found her in some degree of undress, he'd turned abruptly, embarrassed to look, and left the room. It seemed obvious that her husband was now repulsed by her appearance. At a time when the comfort of physical contact would be more than welcome, it was apparently to be denied her. Of course, she'd expected a period of adjustment but Mike obviously had no inclination to make the slightest attempt to improve their relationship, or to give his wife the comfort and encouragement she craved. Did he still somehow blame her? If only she could remember what had happened that morning.

Sue Wainwright was the specialist nurse practitioner who Hannah was due to see. At her last visit, when Sue confirmed that the swelling had gone down sufficiently to measure for the prosthetic leg, she had wrapped Hannah's stump in cling film and applied a plaster cast, after taking numerous measurements and carefully marking out the area around the patella. The pleasant nurse proved to be painstaking in her duties and now smiled at her patient as she entered the room.

'Hi, how are you today?' She spoke warmly.

'Fine thanks ... a little apprehensive perhaps.'

'About anything in particular?'

'I'm just scared that I might not be able to get used to wearing the leg,' Hannah admitted.

'That's quite natural, but I can assure you that it won't be long before it will seem as if the leg's wearing you!' Sue manoeuvred her patient to where she wanted her to be and then took out the new leg. 'Want to have a look?' She handed it over.

Hannah was initially surprised at how heavy it felt but she'd been told that it would weigh approximately the same as her other leg, for balance. She'd had the choice of a solid, natural looking design, or a metal rod with a foot on the bottom, the sort of thing athletes seemed to favour these days, a robotic looking device which some people thought of as 'cool'. Hannah's choice was the natural look and now as she examined it a thrill ran through her at the thought of being able to walk again.

'This is your first prosthesis, one you can wear in the shower if you like, and once you feel confident on it, we'll make another with a softer covering which will look more like flesh. We can make the next one with an articulated ankle too if you'd prefer, which will make wearing heels possible, although not stilettos I'm afraid! But for now let's see how this one fits.'

Sue gave Hannah a cotton sock to pull over her stump, and then she placed the specially fitted 'liner' inside the leg and asked Hannah to place the stump into the prostheses. It felt strange, though not uncomfortable and Hannah began to move her legs around, still seated. She grinned at the nurse.

'Great, now let's try standing up.'

They were only a few steps from the parallel bars and Sue supported Hannah's arm while she tried to move the prosthesis.

'I feel like it's going to drop off!' Hannah said.

'If it feels loose you can try putting another sock on. I've had patients who've worn six or seven socks to get the fit right, and some days you might need more than others.'

Hannah grabbed the bars and positioned herself in between them and started to walk. She balanced rather shakily on her prosthesis and put her good leg forward then dragged the prosthesis up to meet it.

'Try to relax into the leg and then you'll move more naturally. Stand still for a few moments and bend your knees a few times to get used to the feel of it.' Sue watched as Hannah tried to do as she'd suggested.

'I thought it would feel more like a real leg,' Hannah moaned.

'Try to walk naturally to the end of the bars and then we'll sit down again.'

Once they were both seated, Sue looked Hannah straight in the eye and said, 'It's never going to feel like your real leg, Hannah, that's gone, but this will feel good in a surprisingly short time. Your leg muscles need to get used to wearing it and then you'll have the confidence you need to relax and walk normally, which is one of the reasons why we nagged you about exercising your stump in hospital. Once the muscles get used to wearing the leg they'll move automatically and you'll walk more naturally.'

'And I thought I'd be walking out of here today.' Hannah didn't know whether to laugh or cry.

'Goodness no, you'll need to limit your time on the prosthesis initially, probably only a few minutes at a time for the first few days, to get used to wearing it. Even when it's more comfortable, don't overdo it, you'll probably be only too glad to get it off after wearing it for any length of time. Everyone's different and all I can say is to be guided by how you feel. Obviously, if there's any soreness or chaffing, don't persevere, and if you're worried about anything at all give me a ring. If I'm not available there's always someone here who can advise you or see you if needs be. Now, let's have another try, shall we?'

Hannah stood up again, this time knowing what to expect, and moved to the parallel bars unaided. After bending her knees a few more times, she walked the length of the bars with greater ease and finished the short distance with a smile on her face.

'Well done, you're getting used to it already!' Sue grinned. The nurse then went on to talk to Hannah about other aids to help her around the home. Grip bars on doorways and the shower seemed all too sensible, but she was unsure whether she wanted her home to be 'adapted' in this way. These things were just more outward signs of her disability, and she was almost certain that Mike wouldn't like the idea.

With the prosthesis in its bag, Hannah again needed to rely on a porter to take her to reception where she rang for Mike to come and pick her up.

After half an hour's wait he walked in and frowned when he saw her still in the chair.

'What's gone wrong?' he asked.

'Nothing, I just need time to practise using it, that's all. Can we go home now please? I'm tired.'

Still there was no affection or encouragement from her husband and Hannah's mood sank; would things ever get back to normal?

Mel and Sam were both far more enthusiastic for their mother when they arrived home from college later that afternoon. They examined the leg in turn and Hannah explained that this was just her first basic prosthesis and she would eventually get another, possibly with an articulated ankle joint.

'Wow, so you'll be dancing again before we know it!' Mel joked.

'As if I ever could, you know I'm not blessed with a sense of rhythm.'

Mel was keen to see how the leg would fit, and even Sam wanted to stay around to watch. Hannah rolled up her trouser leg and pulled on one of the socks she'd been given to bring home, and then showed them how the liner fitted inside the leg and her stump dropped into it. She then stood up with Sam holding her lightly for balance and took a few tentative steps.

'Brilliant, Mum! Will you be able to wear it all day?'

'Not at first. I'll need to take it slowly to get used to it, but I should be able to build up the time I can wear it and take it from there. You know, walk before I can run sort of thing? Maybe I can think about going back to work now too.'

Hannah was delighted that her children showed an interest in her recovery. They both seemed able to accept the situation far better than Mike could; he had barely looked at the prosthesis when she tried to show him it, saying he needed to get back to work. Maybe when she was walking around more normally he'd find it easier to cope. The accident had made a huge impact on all her family — it was bound to take time for him to adjust, she reminded herself.

CHAPTER 14

Each time Joe thought about his brother over the next few days he did so with incredulity, a feeling which was to be heightened when Joe picked up the post from the mat one morning, noticing a handwritten envelope. It was from David. He let Liffey into the garden then sat down and tore open the envelope.

Dear Joe,

I know we didn't part on the best of terms after Alison's funeral and we would really like to remedy this situation if at all possible.

Joe shuffled uncomfortably in the chair; his brother's letter sounded as if he was writing to a civil servant.

We considered another visit to see you but the truth of the matter is that we cannot afford the petrol; in fact things are so bad at the moment that we may even have to sell the car. I didn't want to trouble you with my problems while you have so many of your own, but we are family and I hope that you can see your way to helping us out of a difficult situation.

It's not that we have been extravagant but were badly advised regarding recent investments and all our savings have been lost. Pam has been quite unwell with all the stress and we find ourselves with credit card debts which are in excess of our modest income.

As your situation has changed and with compensation, and possibly life insurance, coming your way, we wondered if you would consider a loan to enable us to pay off the credit company. £15,000 should cover it. It's not as if your needs will be great now that you're alone and, as I say, we are family and should stick together in times of trouble.

Needless to say if there is anything we can do for you, we will be happy to help.

Your brother,

David

Joe could hardly believe what he'd just read. David's letter was incredible, but went some way to explaining his brother's interest in any future plans Joe might have regarding selling the house, and any possible insurance pay-outs. To casually suggest a figure of £15,000 as if it was nothing, was unbelievable and Joe didn't know what to think. His immediate response was to say a resounding 'no' to his brother, but perhaps it would be better to wait until he calmed down before making any decision; he knew only too well that that would have been Alison's sage advice.

Joe remembered a time shortly after he and Alison were married when his brother asked for a loan of £500, quite a large sum in those days. His initial response then was to refuse; they didn't have much spare cash themselves after buying their first home, but his new young wife persuaded him to hand over the money, as their happiness was overflowing and she was only too happy to share it.

The money was never repaid, which possibly contributed somewhat to the cool relationship between the brothers over the years, and Joe had little doubt that the loan David was asking for now would also not be repaid.

Putting the letter aside, Joe set about preparing a meal in an attempt to take his mind off it. He'd been slowly trying to increase his efforts at domesticity, knowing that he couldn't rely on Phil and Helen's generosity forever, and he anticipated becoming more capable as his shoulder healed. The following day he was again to attend the hospital for another X-ray, which would hopefully show more improvement. His arm was moving without much pain now, although he was still cautious, not wanting to hamper recovery, yet also impatient to be able to drive again and even get back to work.

By 10.30 the following morning, Joe was in the X-ray department, waiting his turn. He'd travelled by taxi, as Phil was working, and would ring for another one to take him home after his appointment. The radiologist worked quickly and efficiently and soon Joe was in another waiting area, in line to see the consultant.

'Excellent,' was the verdict, and both men smiled.

'Can I leave the sling off now?' Joe asked.

'Yes, but don't overdo things. It might be a good idea to wear the sling for an hour or two at some point during the day to give your arm a rest, but if you're sensible and are guided by how you feel, I think we can discharge you today.'

'What about driving? Am I okay for that?'

'Again, if you feel comfortable and don't drive for lengthy periods, you should be fine. Will you be going back to work?'

'Yes, they've been very good and haven't put me under any pressure but I think I'm ready to return now.'

'It's not heavy work you do, is it?' the doctor asked.

'No, I work for an engineering company as a manager in the finance department, nothing physically strenuous.'

'Good. If you do experience any problems don't hesitate to come back. You needn't go to your GP for a referral, just ring my secretary and I'll be happy to see you again.' The doctor smiled and offered his hand to Joe who shook it and thanked him before leaving the room.

As he walked down the corridor his first thought was a reflex ... he'd ring Alison and tell her that he'd been discharged! Even as the idea ran through his mind, the stupidity of it hit him hard. How long would it take to really accept that she was gone?

Once back at home, Joe began drafting a reply to his brother. It was a difficult letter to write, yet he didn't want to ring, wishing to reply in the same manner his brother had approached him. Initially, Joe had been angry at David's insensitive request for a loan so soon after Alison's death, but on reflection he felt a degree of sympathy for his elder brother. His own life must have seemed charmed in comparison to David's, until now of course, and he knew that his brother had never achieved the success he felt he deserved.

In the past, Joe had shown little sympathy for situations which were obviously of David's own making, but now he could almost hear Ali's voice urging compassion and reminding him that this was his brother, his only living relative. He did intend on refusing the loan and pointing out that there was no compensation, or life insurance, as they mistakenly assumed, but for Ali's sake he would try to let them down gently and leave the way open to maintain contact now that they were once again in touch. Perhaps when things were more settled he would send them a few thousand as a gift, but he'd not mention that for the time being.

CHAPTER 15

It felt unbelievably good for Hannah to be walking unaided again. Naturally, it had taken time to adjust to her prosthesis and she still needed regular breaks from wearing it, but Hannah felt human again and was beginning to regain some of her confidence. The twins were a great encouragement and applauded her efforts to walk normally, and more importantly, Mel seemed to have abandoned the crazy notion of giving up going to university to care for her mum. They were in the middle of A-Levels now and Hannah was glad she'd regained some of her independence, not wanting them to be worrying about her at such a stressful time.

Mike, too, seemed relieved that she no longer needed as much help in everyday matters, but his relief manifested itself in his slipping back into his old ways, working too many hours and staying away from home far more often than Hannah would have liked. However, a semblance of normality descended on their home and, although she still grieved for her missing leg, Hannah woke up each morning with a determined, if at times forced, positivity.

A week after getting her prosthetic leg, she walked into the estate agents' office, her place of work, with a smile on her face and was greeted by a round of applause from her colleagues. It was great to be back, although the senior partner insisted that she initially worked only part time, an arrangement which gave Hannah the chance to ease back in gradually.

The office was in the throes of a merger with another local estate agent, an exciting time, most of which she'd missed out on due to the accident, but Hannah was now becoming fully involved with the changes. They were shortly to be moving into larger premises and Hannah, authorised with a generous budget, was given the task of deciding which office equipment and furniture they should take and what should be replaced, in keeping with their move up in the world.

It was a desk-based task but one she tackled with relish, throwing herself back into the work, so absorbed that at times she even forgot she had only one leg, until she moved without thinking and her prosthesis dragged her back, necessitating a conscious effort to walk with it. *How much we take for granted*, Hannah thought, *until it is cruelly snatched away from us*.

Arriving home after lunch on a Tuesday afternoon in late May, Hannah was surprised to find Mike waiting for her in the living room.

'Hello, love, I wasn't expecting you until tomorrow. Plans changed, have they?' She was suddenly anticipating a quiet evening at home with her husband and mentally wondering what she could make for tea.

'You could say that. Sit down, Hannah; I need to talk to you.' Mike's expression was grave, making her wonder what on earth could have happened.

'What is it, what's wrong?' She searched his face but couldn't read his thoughts and he was avoiding eye contact.

'I can't do this anymore.' Again he couldn't look straight at her.

'Do what — what are you talking about?'

'You must know. Us, the happy family bit... it's all wrong, Hannah, and I want out.'

'Is this a joke of some kind, Mike, because if it is, it's not very funny!'

'It's not a joke. Surely you know that things haven't been right between us for months?'

'Is it because of this?' She laid her hand on her thigh. 'I know it's been difficult for you but I'm managing so much better now...'

'No, it's not that. Things were all wrong before the accident. I was on the point of leaving before it happened ... and then, I tried, Hannah, I really did, but I just don't love you any more, I'm sorry.'

Hannah couldn't believe this was happening. Of course things weren't as they'd been in the early years of their marriage, but life changes, relationships change.

'But what about the children, are you telling me you want to leave us all?'

'Yes, that's exactly what I'm saying. The kids are grown up now, they don't need me and they're off to uni soon. I've not been happy for a long time and its surely better that we split up now while we're young enough to make a fresh start.'

'A fresh start! Mike, is there someone else?' The thought hit Hannah like an avalanche. Of course there was someone else, the staying away from home all those nights, not wanting to have sex with her, it all added up and she felt suddenly very stupid, very naive. How could she not have worked this one out for herself?

Mike didn't answer her and looked away.

'Is there, Mike? Tell me. I want to know!' she demanded.

'Yes, there is.'

'How long?'

'We don't need to do this, Hannah, all the sordid details. It doesn't matter how long, I'm leaving and I think the sooner the better.' He turned from her and went upstairs.

Tears were streaming down Hannah's cheeks as she hauled herself up after him. The stairs were still a challenge, but she was determined to know exactly what had been going on, how big a fool she'd been. In their bedroom she was shocked to see Mike's case open on the bed and almost full. A holdall was on the floor already packed. He was going, her husband was really leaving her!

'It's probably just an infatuation, Mike!' She hated the note of pleading in her voice but surely twenty years of marriage was worth trying to save. 'If you've only just met her it might not last, please let's talk about it?'

'I haven't only just met her. It's been two years now and I love her, I want a divorce, Hannah, so I can marry her.' He kept his face turned away.

'So you don't love me anymore, is that what you're saying, and the kids?' She knew she was sounding desperate — but two years, she couldn't believe it, how had she not guessed before now?

'Of course I still love the kids and I'll always be fond of you, Hannah, but I love Sarah and —' He stopped suddenly and turned to look at her. 'Look, I'm leaving tonight. I'll stay and see the kids, you shouldn't have to tell them alone, but my mind's made up, I'm sorry.'

Hannah had a sudden impulse to whip off her prosthesis and whack Mike over the head with it. Didn't he think she'd been through enough lately? Couldn't he see that she needed him? She watched in silence as her husband emptied the last of his drawers. *One suitcase and a holdall*, she thought, *it's not much.*

'Where's the rest of your stuff?' she asked.

'I've been taking a bit at a time.' He sounded embarrassed.

'But why do you have to marry her, Mike? What if it doesn't work out, please stay and we'll talk about it, we can get over this.'

'I don't want to stay! I've tried, Hannah, honestly, especially after the accident, but I know its Sarah that I love and ... she's having a baby.'

Hannah flopped down on the bed, stunned. A baby? Mike had never wanted more children! When the twins were two, she desperately wanted another baby, her body was crying out to procreate again, but he refused emphatically, arguing that they already had a boy and a girl; they should be content with that. Reluctantly, she'd agreed, pouring all her maternal instincts into Mel and Sam, they'd always been her world, with Mike too of course.

A sudden thought popped into her mind.

'This woman's tricked you, hasn't she? She's got pregnant to trap you into marrying her! You don't have to do it, Mike, we'll work through it. You can still support the child; I'll accept that, it's only right.'

'No, it's not like that, we want a baby together. Sarah's thirty-six and has never had children, we planned it. When we knew she was pregnant I was going to tell you and leave then, but ... well, the accident put an end to that and I tried to stay, to make it work, but now you're back on your feet and Sarah needs me and that's where I want to be.'

Hannah couldn't believe this was happening, Mike willingly making a baby with another woman? No, it couldn't be true! But he'd just told her it was, and he was leaving.

A deep feeling of humiliation washed over her, she'd begged him to stay. Even if it was only out of pity she wanted him to stay — how degrading was that? Did she really want a man who didn't love her, who had planned a family with another woman?

She stood, mortified at her own pathetic behaviour, and went downstairs. Mike made no move to follow for which she was grateful; Hannah needed to gather her thoughts, to recoup some dignity before the children came home. At least Mike was staying to tell them himself, he could have taken the cowardly way out and left it up to her.

Hannah made coffee and, when Mike eventually came downstairs, she handed him a cup and sat in the lounge.

'We need to decide how to tell Mel and Sam,' she said calmly, more in control now, more rational, 'but it can't be now, they're in the middle of their A-Levels, they need stability.'

It was obvious that Mike hadn't considered this, he'd obviously had other things on his mind, like his lover and their baby. Her thoughts were uncharitable, but that was how she was feeling at the moment.

Her husband took the coffee she offered and stared into it as if it was a crystal ball.

'So what do you want me to do?' he asked.

'Mel's last exam is tomorrow and Sam's is on Friday. If you must go now I'll tell them you're working away, but I want you to come back on Friday night to see them and explain this yourself.'

Mike looked suitably humbled. 'Okay, that seems only fair. Will you be okay for the rest of the week?'

'And what do you care if I'm not?' she snapped.

'I'd hoped we could be civilised about this, for the children's sake if nothing else.'

Hannah looked away, unable to meet his eyes. 'I'll be fine,' she said, knowing she'd be anything but.

Less than a minute after her husband walked out of the door Hannah gave way to the tears she'd been biting back, angry tears, for herself and her children. She had no idea how she actually felt about Mike's revelations, other than stunned. Had she known somewhere in the back of her mind that this was coming? Perhaps she had, and she had to agree with him that things hadn't been right between them for quite some time, but she'd chosen to ignore it, making excuses and hoping that their relationship would improve.

But now what would happen? Did she simply shrug off her marriage like a wet overcoat, or did she fight for it? Did she want to fight for it, or was it the failure which hurt more than Mike's leaving? It was humiliating that her husband had been having an affair for such a long time without her suspecting and now that he had actually gone, Hannah was the one left with the messy job of applying the glue to fix her family; to tell their friends and neighbours and face their pitying looks, speculation, and inevitable gossip.

Putting her own feelings aside, Mel and Sam must be her priority. They too would feel deserted, let down and hurt, by the very parent who should protect them, but then, hadn't she been the one protecting them throughout their childhood? Mike was never truly comfortable in the role of a father, which was why it was so incredible that he'd actually chosen to have a baby with this new love of his.

Hannah's head spun with conflicting thoughts, vacillating between blaming herself and blaming Mike, hating him and longing for him to come running back and tell her it was all a huge mistake and that she was the one he really loved. But that wasn't going to happen and somehow she needed to get through the next few days, pretending that everything was fine, that her heart was not broken into a thousand pieces and she was not the utter wreck she felt inside.

It would be painfully hard, but Hannah would do it, for her children.

CHAPTER 16

Work became Joe's only escape and what was left of his home life centred on his dog. It seemed that those he'd considered their friends were actually more friends of Alison's than his, or was it simply that a bereaved man was something of a dilemma? Most people they'd socialised with were couples and now that he was alone he didn't seem to fit into their tidy social circle anymore.

The exception to this was Phil and Helen who remained steadfast friends and offered practical help as well as emotional support. Helen was forever bringing him food or inviting him in for a meal, her way of showing she cared, and when they looked after Liffey, they made it appear that it was he who was doing them the favour by allowing them to. Such remarkable people are rare and Joe grew to value them for the true friends they were.

At times he wondered how it would have been if he'd been the one to die and Alison was left alone. Undoubtedly she would have handled it better, probably by widening her circle of friends as a coping mechanism, but it wasn't quite so easy for a man. He couldn't join the WI or an embroidery group and he'd never taken to golf or bowls in the way that some men do, so work became his life and Liffey his love.

He could only continue functioning and remain sane by taking one day at a time and forbidding his thoughts to stray any further ahead. Joe felt he'd lost his future with Alison gone, he didn't want to dwell on the weeks and months ahead, they were just a painful existence to get through, alone.

Now that he was able to drive again, Joe knew he had to fill an obligation which he did not relish; he was going to visit Ethel. They'd spoken on the telephone on several occasions and she seemed to have expectations of Joe which he was not able, or willing to meet.

The insurance company hadn't quibbled about his claim and paid the full value of his written off car promptly, enabling Joe to buy another one. The purchase of a new car had always been a time of excitement but not this one, as there was little pleasure in it for him without Ali to share it.

The drive to his mother-in-law's was the first time he'd taken the same route as the morning of the crash, but he steeled himself to do it, reasoning that avoiding those roads would remind him every bit as much as taking them would.

Ethel Palmer lived in a neat semi-detached bungalow, large enough for one and small enough to maintain quite easily. Not that Ethel took responsibility for any of the maintenance, having expected her daughter to run the home for her. Joe occasionally chipped in with everyday practical jobs when necessary, to take the burden off his wife, but generally Ali had been running two homes, their own and her mother's, typically without complaint.

'You're late,' were the first words that greeted Joe when he rang the bell and walked through the door. Glancing at his watch, he retorted that it was only ten minutes after the time he'd said he would be there. Ethel then launched into a list of grumbles which she'd obviously been storing up to get off her chest, finishing by presenting her son-in-law with a lengthy shopping list, which she assumed he would get immediately.

'Have you done anything about getting some regular help, Ethel?' Joe ignored the list she'd pushed at him with her gnarled fingers.

'And have you any idea how much they charge for the kind of help I need?' Ethel retorted.

'But what else do you spend your money on? You're always saying that you never go out anywhere, so why not get someone in if you can't manage?'

'Well, now that you're driving again you can come over to help me.' It was a statement, not a request, one which was anticipated by Joe and for which he'd prepared an answer.

'I'm going back to work on Monday, I won't have the time to come over like Alison did, and keeping my own place is going to be more than enough for me. I won't be able to drive over here regularly.' Joe might have felt guilty if Ethel's sour expression hadn't grown even darker.

'A fine son-in-law you've turned out to be. I've just lost my only daughter and now you say you don't want to help me!'

'I'm not saying I don't want to help, and of course I'll still visit you, but with work and keeping up my own home, there simply won't be time for me to look after you.' He was trying to be fair but also firm. 'I can help with finding a suitable care company if you like and they can do almost anything, from shopping, to cleaning and cooking.'

'If you'd been able to give Alison children then I would have grandchildren to look after me!' Ethel snarled at him with a look of contempt on her face.

Joe was speechless; her words were like a slap in the face and totally out of the blue. When he composed himself, he tried to form a reply without getting angry at his mother-in-law.

'It was our dearest wish to have children, as you well know, but it's hardly fair to say I couldn't give Ali children, we never went down the route of finding out whose "fault" it was.'

'Of course it was your fault but Alison was too gracious to tell you!' Ethel spat the words at Joe.

'I told you, we never found out why we couldn't have children and it's really nothing to do with you.'

'Well, how come she had a baby before she met you then? It was your fault, you see? You're impotent; my Alison was perfectly capable of having a baby.'

Joe sat down, completely stunned and shaking with shock. He looked at the triumphant smirk on Ethel's face and any sympathy he'd ever felt for her deserted him.

'That's a vicious lie,' he said through clenched teeth. 'She would have told me...' Joe's eyes began to fill with tears, a weakness he didn't want his mother-in-law to see. *She has to be lying; Alison wouldn't have kept something like that from me!* His mind swam with questions; he wanted to know if it was true, but he didn't want this woman to say anymore. Joe desperately wanted to get out of her house, but the need to know more won through.

'Well, what happened to the baby?' he eventually asked, hoping it was all a cruel fabrication and he would catch her out in the lie.

'It only lived a few hours, a little girl it was, she had a weak heart.' Ethel was smiling now at Joe's discomfort. He looked at her in disbelief. How could she be so calculatingly cruel?

'Goodbye, Ethel.' He stood and walked to the door, his legs barely carrying him but his determination to get out of that woman's presence supplying the strength he needed.

'But what about my shopping?' he heard her calling after him as he slammed the door.

The drive home seemed interminable. Joe longed for the comfort of his own home, but most of all he longed for Alison to tell him that her mother's words were nothing more than bitter, vitriolic lies.

Parking in the drive, he went inside and straight to the kitchen where he poured himself a large whisky and, taking it into the lounge, sat down to drink it. Liffey jumped up on the sofa beside him, sensing his mood, and they sat together in silence. Joe's mind raced through the past, trying to find any clues which he could have missed, trying to decide if it was possible that Alison could have had a baby and never told him about it.

Ali was twenty-four when they married and he, twenty-five. He'd only known her for three years so it was quite possible that she could have had a baby before they met, but Joe was certain that they hadn't any secrets from each other, or he had been until Ethel's hateful words shook that confidence. It was so out of character for Alison not to tell him something so monumental; he would have understood, whatever the circumstances, and surely she would have known that?

For the rest of the day Joe was unsettled, his mind swimming with speculation as to why Alison had never told him about the baby. The idea that Ethel was lying was still at the back of his mind, but surely even she couldn't be so callous as to make something up just to punish him for whatever sins she felt he was guilty of. Would the old woman really stoop so low?

Joe began to wonder if there was anyone he could ask, a friend of Ali's perhaps, someone who'd been close to her in the years before they met. There was Juliet, her old university friend, who'd also been her bridesmaid, but she lived in Canada now; he could hardly contact her just to ask about Alison's past.

Remembering Juliet brought a pang of guilt as he'd not thought to write and let her know that Ali was dead and he should do so. He knew the two women communicated occasionally, usually by email, so he would have to search Ali's laptop for her address.

Joe again climbed the stairs and entered Alison's sewing room with Liffey close at his heels, as if she knew that her master would need her comforting presence. He carried three empty cardboard boxes and a roll of black plastic sacks; it was time to sort out some of his wife's belongings, but firstly he fired up her laptop, to find the email address for Juliet.

There were over seventy unopened emails, mostly notifications from book groups his wife had been in, or friend requests from Goodreads, nothing important, they could wait or be deleted. He rarely used social media but Alison had a profile on Facebook which she said helped her to keep in touch with friends. Joe had teased her and called it 'virtual curtain twitching'. He'd never considered the necessity to delete someone's presence from the internet before and now he wondered if he should attempt to remove her profiles from these sites, but would it feel like erasing her life?

He made a note of Juliet's email address and turned the laptop off; social media could wait for another day.

He'd decided to start in this room rather than their bedroom. As yet, he had no desire to remove Alison's clothes from the room they had shared, so they still hung in the wardrobe and her toiletries remained untouched in the bathroom. Joe still needed the closeness and comfort of his wife's possessions, and he would often touch her clothes and breathe in her scent, but he also knew that things couldn't stay this way forever.

He looked around the room, the very essence of Alison layering every surface like dust, trying to decide where to begin. Liffey flopped down heavily on the rug, her huge brown eyes watching his every move as if she somehow understood now that her mistress was not coming back and that Joe was doing his best to carry on.

'It's not easy for you either, is it, girl?' He bent to stroke her ears, receiving a lick on his hand for his trouble.

Straightening up, he began with the books, packing them neatly into the largest box, ready for the charity shop. He felt comfort in touching the things Alison had touched and loved, and as he worked he found himself talking to her about each item.

'Someone will appreciate this, love,' he said, and it made the task easier, knowing that this was what she would have wanted.

After a couple of hours, reasonable progress was made and Joe felt a sense of satisfaction. He would ask Helen if she wanted Alison's sewing machine; she enjoyed making things too and the two women had often exchanged patterns and ideas, it would be a small way of repaying her for all her kindness to him.

Joe went back downstairs, made a mug of tea and fired up his own laptop in order to write the email he'd been putting off.

Hi Juliet,

Firstly, I must apologise for not contacting you sooner but sadly my reason for doing so now is to impart bad news. My beloved Alison died in a car crash on 2nd February. I know this will be a shock to you and I'm sorry to be the bearer of such awful news. It was during that horrendous spell of bad weather we suffered at the end of January and the beginning of February. I've never known anything like it before. We were together in the car and involved in a motorway crash which killed three people and left several others badly injured. My own injury was a broken collarbone, painful but quite light compared to others. I was informed that Alison died instantly at the scene and would have suffered no pain.

As you can imagine, life is proving difficult and I miss her so much. Friends and neighbours have rallied round and the funeral was a fitting tribute to the wonderful person she was. I do feel bad about not letting you know sooner but my head's been all over the place and it's only now that I'm remembering people I should have contacted. You were very dear to Alison and I know she missed your friendship but was happy to know that you're well settled in Canada with Graham. I hope he and the children are well. It's difficult to talk about my wife's death, but this next subject has brought even more pain. As you probably know, Ali cared for her mother, visiting two or three times a week and although Ethel and I have never been close, I felt obliged to visit her when my collarbone had healed and I was driving again. It wasn't a great visit. In a fit of what I can only describe as 'pique' she told me that Alison had had a baby before she met me and therefore it was my inadequacies which prevented us from conceiving. You can imagine how hurtful this was, but Ethel refused to give me any more facts other than to say that the baby, a girl, died within hours of birth of a weak heart.

Perhaps you can understand my confusion and puzzlement at knowing this information. I thought that Alison and I knew everything about each other and had no secrets, but this information has shaken me more than I can say and of course without Ali to discuss it with I feel quite distraught. What I need to know is, firstly, is it true and secondly, why on earth didn't she tell me about it? I would have understood if she'd explained but now I find my mind whirring with all kinds of scenarios, wondering who the father was, how she felt about him and would she have still been with him if the baby had lived? I know this is a big ask and the news of Alison's death must be a shock to you, but I'm desperate for answers and you're the only one I can think of who was really close to her in those years before we met. Please be honest with me, Juliet. Whatever you can tell me will in no way change the way I remember Alison, but for my own peace of mind I need to know the truth.

Kind regards, Joe

CHAPTER 17

'But why?' Mel's eyes were bright with tears. 'Other people's parents get divorced but not ours, not you! I thought we were happy...'

Sam also looked on the point of tears but Hannah knew he would restrain himself, always conscious of how he thought he should react, and showing an excess of emotion was something he rarely did.

'It's nothing to do with you two, love; it's between your mum and me,' Mike told them.

'Is there someone else?' Mel asked.

Mike looked away, embarrassed, turning to Hannah for help.

'Yes, your dad's met someone else,' she said, not inclined to make excuses for him.

Suddenly Mel flew at Mike and began to thump him on his chest. 'I hate you!' she shouted.

Sam sprang forward to pull her away and she collapsed onto the sofa into Hannah's waiting arms.

'Well, I still love you...' Mike's voice cracked. 'And I hope that when you get used to the situation you'll both come and see me and Sarah. You'll always be welcome.'

'Never!' Mel shouted. 'How could you do this to Mum? Especially now...'

'It's got nothing to do with the accident, Mel; your dad was seeing Sarah before that.'

Mel shot Mike a look of disgust.

'So when are you leaving?' Sam asked.

'I've moved most of my stuff out already, so I'll not be coming back here to stay.' Mike paused. 'I really am sorry but you're both on the point of becoming independent, and your mum and I just aren't happy anymore. I'll still be your dad and I'll always be there for you.'

'But just not here! Where will you be living?' Sam was clearly shocked and struggling to take in the unexpected news.

'Sarah has a flat in Bankford, about ten miles away, and you can come and visit anytime you want.'

When Mike's car pulled out of the drive, Hannah looked at Mel and Sam.

'I'm so sorry this has happened — it must be such an awful shock to you both.'

'And to you, Mum! How long have you known?'

'Just since Tuesday. He wanted to tell you then but with your exams and everything I asked him to wait until today. You should really be out celebrating with your friends tonight. Sorry if we've ruined that for you.'

'It's not you who's ruined it, it's him! Did you have any idea that he was seeing someone else?' Typically, Mel would want to know all the details.

'No, love, I didn't, and I felt pretty stupid when he told me. I did know he was finding things difficult but I thought it was this leg and everything that's happened since the accident. He said he tried to make it work afterwards but I'm not sure he could have, and if he really loves this Sarah...'

'He might come back.' Sam looked hopeful. 'If things don't work out with her he'll realise that you're the one he really loves.'

'I can't see that happening. He's known her for two years apparently and there's something else which he should have told you. Sarah's going to have a baby.' *They're old enough to know the full facts*, Hannah thought, *even if Mike had been too cowardly to tell them.*

'The bastard! I don't ever want to see him again!'

'Don't say that, Mel! He's still your father and this baby will be your half-brother or sister — you might want to make room in your life for it. These things happen and I know your dad still cares for you. I think you should give him a chance.'

'You're too nice, Mum, but you'll always have us.' Sam put his arms around her in an unusual, but very welcome display of affection.

'Look, let's order a takeaway for tea and then I want you both to go out and celebrate the end of your exams. You deserve it — you've worked so hard and I'm so very proud of you both.'

'We're not leaving you tonight and I don't feel like celebrating...' Mel spoke for them both.

'Nonsense, I want you to go. I thought I'd ask Rosie round later to help me polish off a bottle of wine or two, so I don't want you around to witness my wicked behaviour!'

Rosie was never one to refuse a half share in a bottle of wine, or some girly chatter, and arrived next door within ten minutes of her friend's call. Perceptive as ever, she noticed the pallor and drawn expression on Hannah's face and immediately demanded to know what was wrong. It was a relief for Hannah to pour out the angst of the week to an understanding friend. She had found it an enormous struggle to carry on as usual after Mike dropped his bombshell on Tuesday, but she'd resisted telling anyone until the children knew.

Rosie listened quietly, her silent empathy both encouraging and soothing. When everything was out in the open she sat back and said, 'Well, he's a bloody fool! He doesn't know how lucky he is to have you and the kids; you're a prize for any man.'

'Even with only one leg?' Hannah almost whispered.

'What the hell's that got to do with it? You're an amazing woman, Hannah Graham, and don't you forget it! And as for planning a baby with a woman he's having an affair with, while still married to you ... well, that's just bloody irresponsible. I hope the baby keeps him awake every night and his floozy gets fat, with swollen ankles, and pimples!'

'Oh, Rosie!' Hannah laughed out loud. 'Don't say such awful things. I suppose he couldn't help falling in love with her. These things happen.'

'There you go, making excuses for him already. He doesn't deserve it, Hannah. He'll soon find out which side his bread's buttered and then he'll want to come crawling back, so I hope you'll tell him where to get off. And what about money? You take him for everything he's got, girl! It won't be cheap sending the kids to uni, you know, he'll have to cough up. Make sure you get yourself a good lawyer.'

'Oh, I'm sure he won't be mean about money, he'll see the kids all right, I know.'

'And what about you? All these years you've devoted to him, you make sure you get half of everything he has — more if you can.' Rosie was in full swing now and that was after only one glass of wine.

'There's time to sort all that out, but he will have another baby to support. I can't expect too much from him.'

'Yes, you bloody well can, and I'll be around to make sure you do!'

The conversation continued in the same vein for most of the evening, Rosie's dramatic outbursts making Hannah laugh when she hadn't thought it possible after a week which had been punctuated by tears and feelings of utter despair. Her friend's drunken rendition of Cher's 'Do You Believe in Life After Love?' almost doubled her up. Rose was just the tonic she needed.

When Rosie eventually left, Hannah went upstairs to bed, not wanting the children to see her the worse for wear. For once, she was fast asleep almost as soon as her head touched the pillow.

CHAPTER 18

Joe was actually smiling, but when he realised it, he felt a sudden stab of guilt. He was in his office at work, checking over some figures, when a colleague came in to ask him something. The conversation turned to their respective dogs and Joe recalled his morning's walk with Liffey when she had bounded over the meadow like a kangaroo. She loved the long grass, especially if it was cool and wet. He'd taken pictures on his phone and laughingly showed his colleague.

When he was alone again, Joe experienced what he could only describe as a sense of disloyalty; it was happening more frequently these days, when normalcy slipped into his day and he paid the price with a sudden surge of guilt. But surely it was a good thing to be able to smile, even to laugh again; he wasn't really betraying the memory of Alison by doing so, was he?

There would come a time when he would have to start truly living again, and not only by working and taking his dog out. It was nearly four months since his wife had died and he'd spent most of that time alone, grieving, not knowing what else to do. His conversation with his friend prompted thoughts of travel; perhaps he should get a caravan, or one of those motorhomes, then he could take Liffey off for long weekends and see a bit more of the country.

Joe had often fancied a motorhome but Alison admitted that she liked her creature comforts too much — a warm bath and a hotel when they were away, so she didn't have to do any cooking. He'd be okay roughing it a bit though, and it would be great for Liffey too. The thought gave him something to dwell on and he decided he would start researching it that evening.

Once home, Liffey's enthusiastic welcome was exactly what Joe needed; she brought him one of Alison's slippers, a habit she'd taken up whenever they went out and left her alone. Really, he should get rid of the slippers to save him that little bit of heartache the sight of them brought, but as yet he hadn't, so he thanked Liffey and stroked her silky coat. Perhaps neither he nor his dog was ready to part with the reminders of Alison just yet.

Joe had taken to buying M&S ready meals for one, and removing one from the freezer each morning so it would be defrosted by his return in the evening. With the intention to search the internet later that evening, he first let Liffey into the garden while he heated his meal. After he'd eaten, he grabbed his jacket again to walk his dog before planning to settle down with his laptop.

It was a pleasant, warm evening with the remnants of sunshine low in the sky. Their route would be the same they had taken that morning; the meadow was perfect at this time of year and an acceptable distance for them both to enjoy the walk. Hawthorn trees scented the air, mingled with the pungent smell of wild garlic, and wild flowers bloomed in abundance; swathes of buttercups, ox-eye daisies, red campion, cowslips and so many others, with names Joe didn't remember, although Alison would have known them all; she'd loved the meadow.

Joe smiled at Liffey as she scooted round and round when he picked up her harness, excitement growling softly in her throat.

'Come on, old girl, walk time!' He caught his spinning dog, pulled on the harness, clipped on her lead and they set off briskly from the house.

Liffey was pulling excitedly on the lead, so Joe walked quickly past the houses and down the lane towards the entrance to the meadow. They had nearly made it when he heard a car, making too much noise for the speed limit of the small road.

He automatically shortened Liffey's lead and pulled her closer to his side, expecting the car to roar past him. As the engine noise increased, he turned to look over his shoulder, annoyed with whoever was driving like a madman.

The last thing Joe remembered seeing was the car rising up onto the narrow path, only a few feet away from him. His heart stopped with recognition when he saw his brother behind the wheel. There was no time to shout out before the world spun violently and everything went black.

CHAPTER 19

The weeks after Mike left were some of the most difficult Hannah had ever experienced. Only the presence of Mel and Sam kept her sane, but she was well aware that their departure for university was looming in the not too distant future, and she would have to make the most of this summer before they flew the nest. Her children were obviously making an effort for her too and she loved them even more for it.

After their initial shock at Mike's leaving and their varied expressions of anger at what he'd done to them as a family, they slipped into an unspoken agreement of not mentioning his name around their mother. But Hannah felt duty bound to occasionally talk about her husband; he was still their father and she was sure that he meant what he said about maintaining a relationship with them.

Mike had been in touch every week, suggesting that the twins might like to meet up with him to go bowling, or to the cinema, but if either of them actually answered the phone, they always had a ready excuse to decline his invitations. Hannah wondered if they'd colluded to make a list of 'reasons' why they were not available, as the words seemed to roll off their tongues with such practised ease.

In spite of all he had done, Hannah felt sorry for Mike. Did he really expect the children to readily accept his new situation, and his new girlfriend? And had he actually thought through the effect that having a new baby would have on his 'old' family?

She was presented with the opportunity to ask him these questions when he rang one weekend and the twins were both out.

'Perhaps I didn't realise it would have such an impact on them,' he admitted solemnly. 'They never seemed to want my company when I lived with you, I didn't think it would make such a difference — not being around I mean.'

'They don't take much notice of the furniture in the lounge but they'd certainly miss it if it suddenly disappeared,' Hannah replied without thinking.

'Oh, thanks, so I mean about as much to them as the bloody sofas, do I?' Mike took it completely the wrong way.

'No, sorry, I didn't mean it like that, it was a stupid analogy. It's just that it's a teenage thing, Mike — they take everything and everyone for granted at this age, it's not personal.'

'Well, it feels like it to me! My own kids don't want to see me — how do you think I feel?'

Hannah was suddenly angry. 'I hope you're not expecting me to feel sorry for you?' she retorted. 'You've made your choices, Mike; perhaps you should have thought them through more thoroughly before you left us!' Her anger dissipated almost as quickly as it had risen and she continued in a softer manner. 'Look, you need to give them time to get over the shock. No child thinks their parents will divorce, and for you to have been seeing someone else all this time, and now a new baby on the way, it's quite a lot for them to process. I'll do what I can to help but there are limits, Mike, surely you can see that?'

'Yes, I know and I'm sorry, Hannah. I know I've hurt you and I regret that, honestly I do, but any help you can give with the kids will be really appreciated. They listen to you.'

'Oh, I'm not so sure about that, but they're good kids. I'll talk to them, see what I can do.'

Hannah did try, more than once, but it was too soon for Mel and Sam, and such a busy time for them both too. After their exams were over they began looking for temporary jobs to earn some money for university, both wanting to keep any student loans they would take out to a minimum — a responsible attitude of which Hannah was so proud.

Mel easily got a job in one of the large hotels, as a chambermaid. It was minimum wage but the tips were good and she regularly picked up extra hours covering for staff absences. She seemed to enjoy the work too and typically made a whole new set of friends to socialise with. Sam also managed to secure a job in the local leisure centre, responsible for a variety of activities including lifeguard duties. The biggest bonus for him was the free access to all the sporting facilities, a dream come true for someone so sport obsessed. The downside for Hannah was that she saw less of her children than before, especially at weekends. She could certainly have done with their presence when two letters arrived one Saturday morning in the middle of June.

Hannah often removed her prosthesis when she was alone in the house, occasionally using crutches, on which she was so much more proficient than in the early days. She loved the new independence her prosthetic leg brought her, but it still irritated her at times and it was such a relief to sit down and take it off.

After picking up the letters from the doormat, she did just that. With a cup of tea on the table at the side of the sofa and the new Jodi Picoult novel she'd begun the night before, Hannah eased open the first letter. As soon as she saw the letterhead, a local firm of solicitors, she knew what it must be; Mike had started divorce proceedings. Why it should be such a shock she didn't understand, she knew her husband wanted a divorce as soon as possible in order to marry Sarah, but it hit her hard, momentarily taking her breath away.

As she stared at the wording blurring before her, it suddenly became so very real. Mike was going through with it, no matter how bad he felt about leaving the children.

Hannah swallowed hard as the thought that he must love Sarah so very much flashed through her mind. *I wonder if he loves her more than he ever loved me?* she thought, and then shook her head to rid her overactive mind of such immature thoughts. But the tears that trickled down her face betrayed her feelings. Unsure of whether she still loved Mike, her reaction told her that perhaps she did, a little bit at least. How do you fall out of love with the person you've shared most of your adult life with?

Reaching for her cup, she drank a mouthful of tea, deciding that chocolate was in order. She stood up to fetch the bar of Toblerone from the fridge. The next thing she knew she was on the floor.

'How bloody stupid!' she shouted out loud. How can you forget you only have one leg? With only her pride hurt, Hannah rolled onto her side and reached for her prosthetic leg from the side of the sofa. Pulling it onto her stump, she rolled onto her knees and managed to raise herself up to standing before flopping back down on the sofa. *Forget the chocolate*, she thought, *where's the wine?*

The second letter she opened was much better news. Hannah had assumed when she had the prosthesis fitted that she would be able to drive an automatic car, but had been disappointed when her physio told her that wasn't possible. No matter how well the leg fitted, it was not considered safe to use a prosthetic leg to drive.

The good news, however, was that Hannah would qualify for an adapted mobility car and the letter in her hand was to tell her that it was now ready for her and would be arriving at the garage later that week. It was just the news she needed to offset the shock of Mike's solicitor's letter.

Since going back to work, Hannah had been relying on the generosity of Rosie and a colleague from her office to give her lifts, but this would mean she would regain her independence, she'd be mobile again.

Almost as soon as the smile spread across her face, another thought raced in behind it. Would she have the confidence to drive again? Of course it had been impossible to try since the accident and now she wondered if her nerve would fail her. Part of the problem, she acknowledged, was that she still couldn't remember the accident. Not a single detail of the day's events had returned to her and there was still that nagging doubt in the back of her mind as to whether she was somehow responsible for what happened.

Did she do something wrong which made her, to some degree, culpable for the awful events of that day? Could she trust herself to drive safely again?

CHAPTER 20

Seeing his own brother deliberately trying to run him down had, without doubt, been the most distressing event in Joe's life after losing Alison. David's face, clearly visible, had been bright red, as if he was going to have a heart attack. There had been no time for Joe to register anything else before he was struck by the speeding car.

His memory of events was a little hazy after that but he clearly remembered seeing David, then bouncing on the bonnet before rolling into the hedgerow at the side of the road and losing consciousness. When he did come round his first thought was for Liffey; had she been struck too? But then he realised his dog was licking his face, she was unhurt.

It was only then that the pain registered. It seared through his hip and shoulder when he tried to move and his head felt as if the percussion section of the Halle Orchestra were rehearsing inside his skull. Helpless, Joe stayed still, not wishing to exacerbate any injuries he may have sustained, but far greater than the physical pain was the incredible realisation that his brother had deliberately tried to kill him. He wondered what on earth he had done for his last remaining family member to hate him so much. Trying to think through the fog in his brain, Joe turned to Liffey for help.

'Liffey, fetch Phil, fetch Helen,' he tried.

Liffey licked his face again and tilted her head to one side.

'Go! Good girl, go fetch Phil, fetch Helen,' he repeated.

Liffey barked once and ran in the direction of home. Joe was surprised and fully expected her to bring him back a stick but she was gone too long for that. When she did return it was with both of his neighbours in tow.

'Good girl, good girl, Liffey!'

Once again his friends had come to the rescue. Phil ran back for the car and insisted on taking him to hospital for a check-up. Joe tried to protest but it was futile so he gave in to the ministrations of his friend and, very soon, the staff at A& E too. X-rays confirmed that his hip and shoulder were only bruised and, apart from a slight concussion, swelling and a black eye, Joe was good to go.

'If your fall hadn't been broken by that hedge it could have been a different story,' Phil pointed out on the way home. He wanted to take Joe to the police station to report the incident and the only way for Joe to explain his reluctance to do so was to tell him the truth.

'The man's evil, pure evil!' Phil was shocked. 'You should still report him, he might try again.'

'Well, perhaps we'll have to think of something to scare him off...' Joe said thoughtfully.

'Count me in.' Phil was eager to volunteer. 'Anything to teach him a lesson!'

And so the plan to let David think he'd succeeded in killing Joe took root. Phil and Helen were enthusiastic co-conspirators, although initially Helen favoured involving the police and letting them deal with it, but she was talked round and agreed to play her small part.

They forged legal letters contacting David as Joe's next-of-kin, and informing him of Joe's death. Phil rang David up, and invited David and Pam to inspect Joe's house, as they were the legal beneficiaries to his estate. Phil arranged for David to pick up the keys to Joe's house the following morning.

At midday the next day, Joe heard David's car pull up in the Ropers' driveway. He quickly hid himself upstairs and waited for them to let themselves into his property.

Joe heard his front door being unlocked, and then Pam speaking to her husband.

'I think new carpets will be in order, there's a strong smell of dog in here!'

'We can't rush in and change things straightaway,' David replied, 'it'll look odd.'

'Oh, don't be so cautious. This is the first good thing to have happened to us in years; can't you just relax and enjoy it?'

'No, I can't! We've got to get in touch with the police, remember, it's not a Sunday school picnic you know, we're not out of the woods yet.'

'Come on, I want a better look at that kitchen.'

Joe heard them both move into the kitchen.

'Wow, look at these units,' Pam enthused, 'they must have cost a fortune! And the tiles, I'm going to love pottering in here.'

Joe heard them move back into the lounge.

'Alison certainly had good taste,' David remarked.

'Upstairs now!' Pam replied. 'I hope they've got an en suite, I've always wanted one!'

Joe heard them walk up the stairs and push open the door to the main bathroom. He heard Pam squeal with delight.

'This is even better than I'd hoped,' she said. 'That must be the master bedroom, let's have a look.'

The door was ajar and Pam pushed past David to get in first. She suddenly screamed, making him jump, and turned back towards him, white as a sheet.

'What the hell is it?' David pushed the door fully open to reveal Joe, sitting in the window seat, his solemn face bruised and swollen.

David gasped, staggered backwards, and then stared at his brother.

'No, I'm not a ghost.' Joe spoke in low, even tones. 'Your clumsy attempt to kill me didn't quite go to plan.' He said nothing else, just stared at his elder brother, disappointment rather than hatred in his eyes.

'Now wait a minute, you've got it all wrong! Whatever you're thinking, it wasn't me, I've been ill in bed for the last few days, haven't I, Pam?' David made a feeble attempt to deny his actions and his wife nodded frantically in agreement. 'Surely you can't believe I'd actually attempt to kill you?'

'David, you were as close to me as you are now, I saw you. Please don't take me for a fool.'

Suddenly, Pam threw herself at Joe and wrapped her hands around his neck. 'You bastard! You should be dead!'

David was quick to pull her off. 'Haven't you done enough damage, woman? Joe saw me, he knows!' As Pam shook herself free from her husband's grip David turned to his brother and said, 'Look, you probably won't believe me but I'm actually glad you're not dead. I was stupid and I've hated myself for planning something so despicable. There's no excuse. I've been in a lot of trouble and there are people looking for me, not very nice people, and the pressure's been building up. I saw this as a way out. But it really is a relief to see you alive and whatever you decide to do, I know I deserve it.'

'Shut up, you fool!' Pam shouted at him. 'He could have the police in the next room listening for all we know, he's tricked us into coming here!'

'Enough, Pam! If Joe wants to bring the police into this, I can't say I blame him. We deserve it.'

'What do you mean, "we"? It was *your* doing, not mine!'

David looked at Joe. He mouthed the words, *I'm sorry*, and hung his head.

The doorbell shattered the silence and Joe stood, limping towards the door to answer it. Pam made to grab him again. 'Is that the police?' she snarled at him as David held her back.

'No, it's Phil from next door. He's here to check that I'm okay. I think you'd be wise to bear in mind that both he and his wife know everything that's happened, just in case you have ideas of another attempt.'

Joe slowly and painfully made his way towards the stairs.

'Now what do we do?' Pam hissed at her husband. 'He's probably already told the police.'

David shook his head and followed his brother down the stairs, Pam at his heels.

'It doesn't matter anymore; can't you see it's over?' he said, but she was agitated, ready to fight for what she wanted, still not accepting that they had failed.

Phil was in the hallway, the look of disgust on his face as he looked past his neighbour to David, spoke more than any words could have done.

'Do you want me to do anything Joe?' he asked, eyes still on David.

'No, thank you, Phil, I think we're done here. My brother and his wife were just leaving.'

'Joe...' David began.

'Goodbye, David.' Joe turned his back on him and walked through to the kitchen.

When David and Pam left, Joe turned to Phil and Helen.

'Thank you both for your help, once again. Whatever you said to David on the phone, Phil, you must have been convincing — they didn't doubt your story at all.'

'Yes, I was quite enjoying the subterfuge until the bastard said he'd be putting Liffey in a shelter! I was so tempted to give him a piece of my mind then. That's when I knew exactly what sort of a man your brother was; he has a complete lack of humanity.'

'I think Joe knows that, dear,' Helen reminded him.

'It's okay,' Joe assured him. 'I couldn't agree more, and Liffey's certainly proved she's anything but a dumb animal.'

'Absolutely!' Helen smiled. 'Hearing her barking outside the house and then her insistence that we follow her to you was just like one of those old episodes of *Lassie Come Home*. Well done, girl!' She reached down to stroke Liffey's silky ears. 'Now, are you going to be okay by yourself tonight, Joe?'

'Yes, I'm certain David won't be coming back, and you've done far too much for me already. Besides, I've got Liffey, haven't I?'

CHAPTER 21

Rosie insisted on a trip to the Trafford Centre to take Hannah's mind off the divorce proceedings Mike had so hastily set in motion.

The vast shopping mall was busy, as it usually was on Sundays, and they'd planned which shops they wanted to visit, so that Hannah wouldn't tire too quickly. The walking would be punctuated by a coffee stop and a lunch stop, so it wouldn't be too onerous.

As they approached the central area, they could see a small crowd gathering at what appeared to be a makeshift animal pen which was attracting the attention of several children. Rosie, always curious, dragged her friend closer to have a look at what was going on. A tall man was supervising a group of children who were petting a lively pygmy goat in the pen. Other children sat on chairs, nursing rabbits and guinea pigs, fascinated with finding furry, living things in a boring shopping centre, their huge smiles showing their delight at the welcome interlude.

'Don't forget to wash your hands before you go,' a pretty young woman reminded a brother and sister who at their mother's insistence reluctantly passed a couple of rabbits to another two children who were waiting in line.

'I wonder what this is all about.' Rosie moved to a display board to read the information posted on it. 'Look, Hannah! They're raising money to start a farm for abused and abandoned animals.' As she read more her eyes widened and she reached for Hannah's arm to pull her closer. 'I think you should read this.'

At the beginning of this year, our son, Timothy, was tragically killed in a road traffic accident. Timothy loved life and had a passion for animals, particularly any in need of care. To celebrate our son's life we are working towards opening 'Timmy's Farm', a centre to care for animals in need and to educate children in the care of the creatures for whom we, as human beings, have a responsibility.

Timothy was born nearly sixteen years ago, with Down's syndrome, but during his short life he taught us so much about love and caring for others. Our only child left us far too soon, when we were not ready to let him go, but we know that he would be the first to want to make his life count for something, to build something positive from such a tragedy.

'Timmy's Farm' is an ambitious project but Timothy always dreamed 'big' and we're learning to do the same. We've already been overwhelmed by the generosity and support of many who wish to assist us in the setting up and running of this venture. Links with the Down's Syndrome Association and several children's groups have already been established and many have expressed an interest in using 'Timmy's Farm' to help their members interact with, and learn about our animals. Initially we plan to offer four full time jobs to young people with learning disabilities and our dream is that this number will grow and we can offer animal therapy sessions to as many children who need them.

We already have a number of animals, many of which Timmy had 'collected' and cared for himself. Today we have George, the pygmy goat with us, as well as several of Timmy's chickens, rabbits and guinea pigs. We also care for two elderly donkeys and a Shetland pony, and we receive requests to house other animals in need every week. Please feel free to talk to us about our plans and any help you are able to offer will be gratefully appreciated. Our intention is to have an open day in the autumn. We will be announcing the date in the local press and on social media.

Thank you for showing an interest in our plans.
Alan & Cassie Jones

'I thought that man looked familiar. I remember him from the inquest! Come on, let's go and talk to him.' Rosie began to steer Hannah towards Alan Jones.

'No, I can't!' Hannah pulled away, turning to move in the opposite direction.

Rosie noticed Hannah's distress and she quickly changed direction, hurrying Hannah into a coffee shop.

'I'm so sorry,' Rosie said, once they were seated. 'That was totally crass of me — as usual I stupidly didn't think.'

'No, it's just me being silly. They're doing something so wonderful, but I simply couldn't face them.'

'But why? Did it bring it all back to you, a kind of flashback or something?'

'I don't have flashbacks, I still can't remember anything about that day, it's just...' Hannah found it hard to express her feelings but in halting words it all came tumbling out. She admitted to her friend how she was constantly troubled with feelings of guilt, wondering if she was somehow to blame, if she'd done something wrong and inadvertently caused the accident. Then she shared her concerns about driving again, whether she'd have the confidence, or even if she was safe to drive at all. She remained dry-eyed as she spoke but her face was pale and her eyes dull and distant. When she finally ran out of words, Rosie reached out and covered her friend's hand with her own, squeezing it gently.

'Hannah, the police investigated the accident thoroughly and the coroner ruled that no one was to blame. I know it's easy for me to say, but I also know you. You wouldn't have done anything stupid; you're the most sensible person I know! I've heard you telling people what you think of using a mobile when driving, and drink driving, you're one of the most fastidious drivers I know. And I'm sorry for almost dragging you into a situation where you'd be uncomfortable. I thought you might be interested, that's all.'

'Actually, I am interested, it's simply that I couldn't face them, thinking that their son might have died because of me!'

'No, he didn't! He died because of an accident, which by definition is no one's fault. Anyway, I picked up a leaflet about their plans if you are interested?'

Hannah took the leaflet. She might not have felt comfortable talking to the boy's parents but she was certainly curious to see what they had planned in his memory. As she read through hit, she smiled. 'Timmy's Farm' sounded like a wonderful idea and she resolved to send them a donation, anonymously of course.

CHAPTER 22

After his shocking confrontation with David, Joe was stunned by a second event later that evening. Juliet had replied to his email. He opened up her message and read through it quickly.

My dear Joe,

Your email came as such a shock and I am so terribly saddened to hear of Alison's death. My thoughts and prayers are with you at this difficult time and I'm only sorry I'm not able to offer my help in any tangible way. What I can do, however, is to tell you what happened to Alison in the hope that you'll understand why she never told you about the baby. As far as I know she only ever told her mother and myself, and I have to say that Ethel is (and in my opinion always has been) a bitter twisted old woman who didn't deserve such a caring daughter. I was sworn to secrecy by Alison, but as she is no longer with us I feel certain that she would want you to know the truth, rather than Ethel's distorted version of it, designed no doubt to repay you for whatever wrong she imagines you have done her.

It happened in about the third month of our first year at uni. Alison and I had rooms next to each other in the halls of residence and we became great friends. As with all the other students, we were enjoying our newfound freedom away from the constraints of home, and there were so many new experiences to enjoy which we threw ourselves into. Alison had been kept very much under Ethel's thumb at home and was in many ways quite naive, which sadly made her rather vulnerable. I don't think she'd ever had a boyfriend, so when she was invited out by a third-year student it seemed so exciting. Neither of us knew the boy in question but a date at the cinema seemed innocuous enough and I remember helping her get ready and her anticipation of what was really her very first date. The boy concerned had a car and picked her up from the halls as arranged. I almost envied her, he was rather good looking and confident, quite a catch it seemed, but three hours later a very different Alison was banging on my door. I was horrified to find her bruised and scratched and in a dreadful state. Her 'date' had taken her to the cinema and then driven out into the country, where it seemed he expected 'favours' for his trouble. When Alison resisted, he raped her, quite violently, then drove her back to the halls and dropped her off outside as if nothing had happened. As you can imagine, she was in an appalling state, but when I suggested we went to the police she became almost hysterical. In those days rape wasn't always taken seriously by the police, especially what's now termed 'date rape' and Alison was terrified that she wouldn't be believed, and that telling the police would be like being violated all over again.

I'm sorry, Joe, this must be so very hard for you to read, and I'm sure you know where it's going. Alison didn't report the incident and a few weeks later matters were made so much worse for her when she found out she was pregnant. I tried to persuade her to see a doctor and tell him what had happened, sure that she would be offered an abortion, but Alison was horrified at the suggestion and said that it wasn't the baby's fault and she couldn't punish an innocent child. It was so typical of her. She must have been torn apart, yet she bore it stoically.

When the baby began to show, she left uni and returned to face Ethel. I don't think she ever really told me the half of what she suffered from her mother, who called her a slut and much worse, I'm sure you can imagine. I really can't believe that Ethel would throw this back at you now after all the trouble she gave her daughter at the time. She really is a selfish old witch! Anyway, the rest you apparently know; Alison had the baby and was quite prepared to devote herself to being a single mother, until fate took over and the baby died.

Alison came back to uni to finish her course. I think it was a relief to get away from her mother again. I was in the second year by then and we shared a house with another girl, so I was able in some way to look after *her. She was such a gentle soul and never felt sorry for herself, and she even grieved over the baby.*

After a while we made a pact never to speak of the incident again, and we didn't for a long time; it seemed to be her way of coping with it. The only time I brought the subject up again was a few years later, after she'd met you and you were planning your wedding. As her bridesmaid I felt it right to suggest that she told you what had happened. I didn't know you well but felt sure you would understand. Alison didn't agree, not because she thought you wouldn't understand, but because she didn't want you to be burdened by what she had suffered. To her it was a very deep sadness and one she didn't want you to feel for her. I don't know if I'm explaining this well, but please believe that her motives were pure. She wished only to protect you from the pain of knowing what she had been through.

You have lost a wonderful woman and I have lost a very dear friend. This will be painful for you to learn, I know, and if you want to talk about it please feel free to Skype me at any time, listening is the least I can do for you and Alison.

God bless you, Joe,
Juliet

Joe felt exhausted. It had been quite a day. He had been wondering if Juliet's reply was ever going to come, thinking that maybe he'd been wrong to approach her when she was someone he barely knew. He'd tried not to dwell on his mother-in-law's hateful words, but they were always there, lurking at the back of his mind, ready to assault him at a low point, of which there were many.

The story the email told was incredibly sad, and Alison's wish to protect him by keeping her past suffering to herself, typified his wife's nature. The email answered Joe's questions, but strangely it also brought him comfort. Alison's memory was once again intact and he felt shame at those niggling, disturbing doubts he'd allowed to creep into his thoughts, the scenarios he'd imagined which did his wife no credit and now filled him with remorse.

Initially, he felt a desire to confront Ethel, to tell her exactly what he thought of her; she was prepared to let him think ill of his wife, to besmirch her character just to spite him, a fact which spoke volumes about her own warped character. But Joe was tired. The last couple of days had been incredibly difficult and the events had taken their toll, physically and emotionally. Would he ever come to terms with the fact that his brother had wanted him dead? Perhaps not, but maybe David was more to be pitied than hated. Joe had seen what hatred could do; he was learning to let go of bitterness and resentment. For Alison's sake, he did not want to be the person with a chip on his shoulder, the man with a distorted image of the world.

Joe needed to take a few days off work to recover from his injuries. He telephoned in, admitting to an accident, without going into details. His head throbbed constantly and his shoulder and hip were stiffening, causing pain when he moved, so a few days' down time would probably be good for him. He would rest and exercise gently by walking Liffey over the meadow, taking the car to the gateway to cut down on the walking. There would be time to sort out some more of Alison's things too, not an easy task, but one he was accomplishing in stages.

Reading Juliet's email once again, Joe allowed tears to fall for his wife's sufferings, yet the image he held of her in his mind was of a vibrant, loving person. He knew that she would want him to live, not simply to exist. He would write to Juliet and thank her for her honesty and to let her know how much it had helped him.

The next morning, Joe woke early, his head pounding and his body aching. Liffey was on the bed beside him, her chin resting only inches from his face, looking hopefully at him with those doleful, irresistible eyes. With slow, deliberate movements he rolled out of bed and made his way to the bathroom; he was feeling even worse than the day before, his limbs were stiffening up and every movement was an effort.

Taking the stairs slowly, he made it to the back door and let Liffey out; she would have to see to herself until Helen arrived to take her out for a run. Briefly, he wondered how his brother was feeling this morning. David had expressed a modicum of remorse, but Joe was uncertain how genuine the sentiment was; perhaps it was only an act to dissuade him from involving the police?

But his brother wasn't his problem anymore, and Joe doubted that he would ever hear from him again. Leaving the back door open for Liffey to come in when she was ready, Joe limped back upstairs and stood under the shower for a full fifteen minutes, letting the warm jets of water massage his aching body.

Getting out, feeling refreshed and more mobile, he dressed and went about the early morning tasks of feeding himself and Liffey. As well as thoughts of his brother and the events of the previous day, Juliet's email was at the forefront of his mind. It had answered so many questions but also given him much more to think about. Ethel's role in it all was certainly a black one, and anger simmered to the surface of his mind as he thought about how she had shown very little compassion during Alison's time of need. More recently Ethel had used her daughter as an unpaid carer, and was even now prepared to besmirch her memory in order to score points against Joe. What an incredibly selfish woman she was!

Helen arrived to take Liffey for a walk and fussed over Joe as much as he'd allow her to. When Liffey was returned and the house was in order, Joe sat in the conservatory with a coffee, intending to do nothing more until lunch time and he very quickly drifted off to sleep. The telephone woke him and he was surprised to see that it was after 1pm.

'Good afternoon, is that Mr Joe Parker?' a man's voice enquired.

'It is, yes.'

'Ah, hello, this is Detective Sergeant Ted Armstrong from Hampshire Constabulary in Eastleigh. Could I confirm whether or not you are a relative of Mr David Parker?'

Joe's heart sank. What could possibly have happened now?

'Yes, I'm his younger brother. Is anything wrong?' he asked.

'I'm very sorry to have to tell you that your brother is dead, Mr Parker. We found your number in a phonebook at his flat and I wonder if I could ask you a few questions? Again, I'm sorry for your loss and for having to inform you on the telephone like this, but circumstances dictate that we act swiftly.'

'That's okay; it's just a bit of a shock, that's all... How did he die?'

'It appears that a domestic incident got out of hand. Could you tell me the last time you saw your brother, Mr Parker?'

'Um, yes, I saw him yesterday actually.' Joe's mind raced; should he tell the sergeant everything? And what did he mean by a domestic?

'Yesterday?' The sergeant sounded surprised. 'Did you visit him here?'

'No, David and his wife came here to visit me but only for an hour or so...'

'A four-hour drive for an hour's visit seems a little unusual.'

'Yes, I agree. Look, I'm sorry, sergeant, but by a domestic do you mean that Pam has killed David?'

'We have arrested Mrs Parker on suspicion of murder, but you don't seem too surprised at that.' The sergeant was picking up on every nuance of Joe's answers. There wasn't time to think through what to tell him, he'd just have to tell the truth.

'The thing is, I'm actually recovering from a recent accident, well no, it wasn't an accident. I think there's something you should know about my brother...'

CHAPTER 23

Rosie took Hannah to collect her mobility car and, after a brief lesson from the mechanic at the garage, her friend sat with Hannah while she drove for the first time since the accident. It wasn't easy but the desire to regain her independence spurred her on, to be able to ferry her children around once more and for them to rely on her rather than the other way around was her goal. Rosie encouraged and applauded her, insisting that they drove on the motorway, although not yet to the site of the accident, and it paid off.

After over an hour, Hannah's confidence returned and she began to enjoy the feeling of being in control, even if the actual driving was different from what she was used to. She liked the car and found it easy to manage and had to admit that it was going to make her life so much easier, especially as she was back working full time again. Her car had been essential to her before the accident, but now that her mobility was impaired it was even more crucial; using a bus was now an impractical option, as walking to and from bus stops was difficult and even painful at times. Hannah would enjoy her regained self-sufficiency; it was one step more to living a 'normal' life again.

One of the first places Hannah visited in her new car was a solicitor's office. With more than a little reluctance, Hannah had engaged the services of a local firm who had been recommended to her. She'd begun to accept that her marriage was over for good and there was no reason for her to contest the divorce. Mike was never coming back and she didn't want to be stubborn simply out of spite.

Hannah found a parking space with relative ease, just a short walk from the solicitor's office, which was housed in an old Victorian building, carved up into commercial units. Thankfully, Ms Emily Cowan had her office on the ground floor. As Hannah was early, she perched uncomfortably on one of the plastic bucket seats to await her appointment, listening to the high-pitched sing-song voice of the receptionist repeating the same sentence to every caller.

Eventually, Emily Cowan appeared in the doorway and invited Hannah into her office. A plush chair and air conditioning greeted her, a welcome relief on such a hot day. Emily Cowan was younger than Hannah had expected, mid-thirties she would guess, and she had rather pinched features, but her smile softened the effect.

'Now then, Mrs Graham, I believe your husband has filed for divorce?'

Emily Cowan opened the conversation and got straight to the point. Hannah was relieved; Rosie had spent the last evening drumming instructions into her, the most important was to be succinct as solicitors charged by the hour and she was warned not to waste time with chit chat.

Hannah fumbled in her bag for Mike's solicitor's letter and handed it over. Emily Cowan skimmed the page and put it to one side, on top of a manila file — Hannah's divorce file.

'It's pretty standard. As your husband admits to an affair it should be a straightforward case. Have you got your marriage certificate with you?'

'Oh, no, I never thought...'

'Well, if you could drop it into the office some time?'

'Yes, of course, sorry.' Hannah then listened to her solicitor outlining the process, and wondered how many times she had done this before. What a depressingly sad job. When it came to the matter of joint property and the financial settlement, Hannah explained that she didn't want to ask for any more than what was reasonable. Mike had his new partner and a baby to consider and she was earning a good wage.

Emily Cowan looked up from her notes to stare at her new client, one eyebrow raised, and a look of surprise. She then commenced a little speech, one which she'd probably used several times before, about how Mike had had nearly twenty years of Hannah's life, she had looked after him and their children, and now he was discarding her, with no more thought than if she was an old newspaper.

Hannah squirmed, feeling like a naughty schoolgirl but as she listened, she became increasingly irritated. This woman didn't know what her marriage had been like; surely divorces were not 'one size fits all', were they?

'Actually, I know all the clichés, the best years of my life and so forth, but this is how I want it to be, civilized, and I'd rather err on being generous, so that our children have a good example and don't see their parents fighting over money.'

Why did everyone think life was all about money? Hannah had enough for her needs and always considered herself fortunate. Her dignity was more important than getting what she could from a settlement.

'That's fine then.' Emily Cowan's features again softened and she abandoned the stock speech. 'You're the client and I'm happy to do whatever you wish.'

The air had been cleared and Hannah remained only long enough to answer all the necessary questions which would allow her solicitor to respond to the petition, then she left, promising to drop in the marriage certificate the next day.

When she got home, Hannah opened her laptop and spent half an hour reading the Facebook page for Timmy's Farm. She couldn't help being impressed. It was packed with photographs showing the progress to date, a visual diary of just how busy Cassie and Alan Jones had been. What they'd achieved in just a few short months was amazing, and it was apparent that their home was ideally suited to the purpose they were working towards.

Being faced with the photographs of their son was, however, difficult for her. He was a smiling boy, face covered with freckles and a mass of red hair flopping into bright green eyes. He'd had everything to live for and should have had years of happiness ahead of him. Hannah fought back tears and the now familiar, unwelcome feeling of guilt which she still could not shake off. The decision of the coroner and the opinions of her family and friends all emphasized that her guilt was irrational but until she could remember the accident for herself, it would remain firmly lodged at the back of her mind.

But would she ever remember? Seeing Timothy, so vivacious and animated, it was difficult to believe that he was dead, and if she felt that way, then Hannah could only imagine the heartbreak his parents must be battling with each day.

Timothy's love for animals was patently obvious; there were images of him with his chickens, apparently rescued battery hens, the pygmy goat called George and various other animals and birds. The Jones's had certainly found a fitting project as a memorial to their son, and their hard work and dedication was evident in every photograph and post.

There were also accounts of others who had helped by donating money or by various practical means. Over ten thousand pounds had been raised by the pupils at Timothy's school, through a sponsored walk, and they had pledged to hold at least one fundraising event each year to help the continuation of the work.

Hannah found all the accounts humbling and had no hesitation in turning to the 'Just Giving' page to make her own generous donation; she too felt the desire to support this amazing project which would be a living tribute to a remarkable young man. Seeing the photographs and reading the accounts not only inspired and humbled her, it gave pause for thought as to her own life since the accident. True, she had lost her leg, but not her life, her husband, but not her children. When dark moods and moments of self-pity crossed her mind, Hannah vowed to think of Timothy and his parents and be grateful for the blessings she still had.

CHAPTER 24

DS Ted Armstrong was a tall, wiry man, about forty years old and almost completely bald. He arrived late morning on the day after his telephone call, alone, which surprised Joe, and with an easy, almost languid manner, he began to prise out the information he wanted.

Joe had asked Phil and Helen to be with him at the interview, as the sergeant would almost certainly want to speak to them and hear of their involvement in recent events, and being Saturday, it was no problem for them both to be there. He appreciated the moral support, too. When he broke the news that David was dead they were understandably shocked, and Joe was concerned that he may somehow have landed his friends in trouble by involving them in his plans.

Helen made coffee and after the detective once again offered his condolences, they sat in the lounge, awkwardly taking the measure of each other.

'Mr Parker,' DS Armstrong began, 'from what you told me on the telephone yesterday, your brother attempted to kill you a few days ago, yet you decided not to report this to the police. Can you tell me why?'

Joe had tried to explain on the phone, but now he supposed he must go over all the details again.

'Yes, I've no doubt that it was an attempt to kill me, but David was still my brother and whatever he'd done, I couldn't bring myself to report it and possibly see him sent to prison.'

'And with your neighbours here you hatched a plan to teach him a lesson?'

'You could say that, but it was entirely my doing. Phil and Helen agreed to go along with it but only after they tried, unsuccessfully, to persuade me to tell the police.' Joe wondered what charges the police could bring against him; surely there'd be something.

'And your brother and his wife just left after learning that you were still alive?'

'Yes, I assumed they were going home, as it appears they did.'

'When you saw your brother in the car when he drove it into you, was he alone?' Armstrong asked.

'Yes, as far as I could see, but it all happened very quickly.'

'So as far as you know his wife wasn't with him that day?'

'That's right, but I've no doubt she was part of his plan, if not the instigator of it.'

DS Armstrong turned his attention to Phil. 'And you, Mr Roper, did you witness Mr Parker's brother's attempt on his life?'

'Well no, but Liffey came to fetch us, that's the first we knew about it, when we found Joe in the ditch down by the meadow.'

'And this Liffey is?' The sergeant looked puzzled.

'The dog.'

Armstrong glanced over at Liffey who was snoring gently in the corner of the room. 'Right, the dog. So when the dog took you to the scene what happened next?'

'I took Joe to the hospital but he didn't want to go to the police.'

Joe was becoming a little frustrated with the questions and wanted a few of his own answering. 'DS Armstrong, unless you intend to charge me with failing to report a crime, I don't see where your questions are leading. So far you've told me very little about what happened and I'd like to know exactly how my brother died.'

The detective shifted his weight in the chair and nodded. 'Right, of course, but I'm afraid it's not pleasant.'

'Death seldom is, my wife died five months ago and now my brother, and I'm feeling as if I'm under suspicion here.' Joe was feeling bolder; he'd done nothing wrong and wanted to know what was going on.

'I'm sorry to hear that, Mr Parker, and I apologise if you feel that way. I assure you that you're in no way under suspicion. Your brother died from stab wounds, several punctures in what must have been quite a frenzied attack. If it's any consolation, death would have been very quick; most of the wounds appear to have been inflicted post mortem.'

Helen gasped and her hand flew to her mouth. Phil wrapped a comforting arm around her, a frown on his face.

Joe felt sick. His brother might have done some terrible things but he didn't deserve this. Pam must be completely mad.

'And it was Pam who killed him?' Joe asked.

'We've arrested Mrs Parker on suspicion of murder. There was a call from a concerned neighbour about noise from their flat and when our officers arrived they found your brother. Mrs Parker was soon picked up and there is evidence which ties her in to the incident.'

'So why all the questions about David's attempt to run me over?'

'Well, if you wish to press charges, obviously not against your brother, but against Pamela Parker, we can add that charge to the one of murder.'

'What, conspiracy?'

'Yes, something like that.'

'But surely that would be virtually impossible to prove, especially now that David's dead?'

'That's certainly true, but it's a matter of building up the pressure on our suspect. If she feels there are other charges in the offing, she may come clean about the murder.'

'What, you mean the woman's trying to say she didn't do it?' Joe was astounded.

'Exactly.'

'Bloody hell, she must be insane!'

'And I think that's probably going to be her line of defence.' It was the most forthcoming thing Armstrong had said, and he reluctantly agreed to leave Joe to think about pressing charges. 'We'll keep you informed as to how the case is progressing, Mr Parker, and if you'd like to discuss anything with me this is my direct line.' He handed Joe a card and left, uttering more condolences.

'My goodness, they must be trained in stock phrases at copper school!' Phil remarked when he'd gone. 'What are you going to do, Joe?'

'I haven't a clue. They seem to think that I should be sorting out the flat and everything, all that talk about when the "crime scene" is released. It's the same bloody roundabout all over again, isn't it?' Joe was close to tears.

'I wouldn't count on that, mate. Perhaps you should seek legal advice; surely no one can force you to take responsibility for their affairs, especially in the circumstances.'

'Don't get in a state about it, Joe,' Helen chipped in. 'I should think the investigation will take some time, there must be some protocol for these situations, or if nothing else you could just put the flat in the hands of house clearers, or leave the landlord to do so.'

'I'll have to arrange a funeral for him. It's a hell of a way to die and he was family...'

'You should wait a few days, see what this Armstrong comes back with. There's no urgency and you're not in any fit state to be arranging anything at the moment.' Joe could tell Phil was concerned for him.

'You're right,' Joe agreed. 'It hasn't really sunk in yet. I can't believe that she could actually do that to her own husband, it's barbaric.'

'Now, no arguments, you're coming round to ours for some lunch,' Helen insisted, 'and Liffey too. It's only cold ham and salad but you don't have to stay. Come back home when you want to, you need to rest.'

Joe was in no mood to argue and accepted his friends' ministrations, glad of their presence. He would do as they suggested, think things over, and then talk to the detective when he felt better. Nothing he could do would help his brother now.

CHAPTER 25

The lethal combination of freezing rain and wind battered the windscreen so hard that Hannah feared it might shatter, the violent pounding was deafening, frightening. Suddenly, the car seemed to shift of its own volition, it veered ever so slightly to the left and she tried to counter the shift by turning the steering wheel to the right. But the car had taken on a mind of its own; she was no longer in control. Fear swelled inside her, cold as the ice outside, as the momentum gathered and Hannah was carried along inside the prison of her car, utterly helpless as it descended the gradient, sliding uncontrollably towards the inevitable. She saw an articulated lorry approaching from the right and her car suddenly fishtailed, like a ride at a fairground. There was an explosive boom, the horrified faces of a man and a woman, and the piercing sound of Hannah's own voice, an impotent scream, and then nothing. Dark, interminable silence.

Hannah couldn't breathe; it was as if all the oxygen had been sucked out of the room. She sat up, her nightdress soaked with perspiration, her jaw stiff and twisted, and her fingers clawing at the sheets. On one level she knew that she was awake and in her bedroom but in the disorientation which so often follows sleep, she was inside her little Ford Focus. The room was hot but she felt as cold as the ice had been on that fateful day.

Was she dreaming, or was she actually remembering those events which her mind had so stubbornly blocked from her consciousness? Looking at the clock, the digits flashed 4.30am and she knew there would be no more sleep that night. The house was silent; the twins must still be sleeping, so the scream, which had been so real to her only moments ago, had probably just been in her head.

When Hannah's breathing slowed and the blood stopped pounding through her temples, she reached for her prosthesis and pulled it on. She made her way downstairs and into the kitchen where she occupied her trembling hands with the mundane task of making coffee. A shiver ran through her body, and even though the early morning sun had already warmed the kitchen to a comfortable temperature, it was as if ice was running through her veins.

Wrapping her hands around the hot mug soothed her and she began to think rationally, analysing what had just happened. Had it been a dream, or was she remembering the accident? How the hell was she supposed to know the difference? Could it be what they call 'false memories' or just a dream based on other people's accounts of what occurred that day? Her mind was spinning, and she was unsure what to think, what to believe.

As the caffeine reinvigorated her body, her mind began to clear. The images had been too vivid to be only a dream and now as they again played through her mind, Hannah became convinced that she was experiencing a memory.

In her mind's eye, she saw herself leaving for work that morning, exchanging a few words with Rosie and hurrying into the car, out of the bitter cold weather. These were things no one else could have told her, they must be genuine memories. Up until this 'dream' she hadn't even remembered speaking to Rosie that morning but now she could even recall what their brief exchange had been about and how bad she felt at letting her friend down.

A mental picture of herself, down to what she was wearing that morning, lodged in her mind; she couldn't have heard that at the inquest. She remembered it all, the panic of being thrust towards the motorway, the unresponsive brakes of the car and the sheer terror of being powerless to prevent the inevitable. The movements of her car felt like a ballet being danced in slow motion, a deadly choreography which she was powerless to stop, but the approaching vehicles on the motorway were travelling at speed.

Hannah braced herself for the collision, her little Ford Focus spinning round as it reached the motorway, and smashing into the back of a lorry. For a split second everything was still. She became suddenly aware of the terrified faces of a man and a woman heading straight towards her, and then everything went black.

It was a memory, a sombre, mournful memory but also a relief. *It hadn't been her fault!* The more Hannah thought about it, the more she could see that there was nothing at all she could possibly have done to prevent the sequence of events that had occurred that morning. The control of her car was irrevocably taken out of her hands; she was at the mercy of the elements, as was everyone else involved in the collision. Fate took over, remorseless fate, cruel, harsh, severe.

Hannah couldn't possibly have prevented the accident and there was nothing she had done to cause it either. It was as if a weight was suddenly lifted from her as she sat at the kitchen table and actually smiled. For the first time since the accident she knew with certitude that she had no culpability in the awful events of that day, a certainty she'd longed for. The knowledge brought with it freedom and she knew that she could now go on living without the burden of guilt and shame which had haunted her since the accident. She was at last released from such debilitating emotions.

Hannah had no idea how long she had sat there but when Sam appeared in the kitchen doorway she grinned at him.

'It's only six o'clock, Mum, what are you doing up?'

'Couldn't sleep; what's your excuse?'

'I'm on early shift at the centre. Any chance of a lift, seeing as how you're up?'

'I can think of nothing I'd like to do more than give my handsome son a lift to work! Grab some breakfast while I get dressed!'

CHAPTER 26

It took almost two weeks for Joe's bruised and swollen face to look anything like normal again. The colours changed from yellow to black, then yellow again and his hip and shoulder were still quite sore. Taking Liffey out was good exercise, although he slowed his pace accordingly, as he didn't want to seize up and he'd had enough of recuperating after the accident in February.

If he didn't keep busy, Joe's thoughts ran away with him. It would be so easy to fall into the trap of self-pity after the dramas which had befallen him of late but he steadfastly refused to go there. The year was certainly turning out like no other he'd ever experienced. Losing Alison was more than enough to bear but David's murder had also hit him hard.

It was still an ongoing investigation, but the police had charged Pamela with the stabbing and it looked as if it she might even confess. When he received another call from DS Armstrong wanting to interview him again, he could no longer put off a visit to Eastleigh. Joe was hoping that his involvement might simply amount to arranging the funeral, but he was aware there was the matter of the flat to consider.

The drive was uncomfortable as Joe's hip was still sore but he'd decided to travel after work on Friday night; he'd already taken more time off work than he'd have liked, and the traffic was mercifully light. He'd arranged to meet DS Armstrong at 9.00am on the Saturday; and so he'd booked a room in a Premier Inn for the night.

The hotel was clean and comfortable and surprisingly Joe slept like a baby, thoroughly exhausted.

After a hearty breakfast in hotel restaurant, Joe set off to meet DS Armstrong. There was no police station in Eastleigh, so he travelled the five miles to Southampton Central, where the detective was based. He was greeted cordially and offered coffee, which he accepted gratefully, and then Armstrong began to update him.

'Mrs Parker has pleaded guilty to manslaughter, her plea being that her mind was disturbed due to her husband's constant abuse.'

Joe was shocked. 'Constant abuse? Is she trying to say that David abused her throughout the marriage?'

'Yes, apparently. She's citing physical abuse and mental cruelty.' Armstrong watched Joe carefully for his reaction, and then asked, 'Do you buy that?'

'No! I can't claim to have been close to David, especially in later years, but I'm pretty certain that he wouldn't have been violent towards her.'

'You think that, even though he tried to kill you?'

'I know it seems incongruent, but if you'd told me it was the other way round, that she abused him, I'd find that much easier to believe. During our last encounter, David appeared almost penitent for his actions, she was certainly the more hostile of the two, and I got the distinct impression that she'd been the driving force behind his attempt to kill me.' Joe couldn't be certain but that's the way he'd read it at the time.

'Sadly impressions count for nothing in a court of law, Mr Parker. Her defence will be thorough and the prosecution are currently looking for witnesses to disprove her story, but rather unsuccessfully, I'm afraid. Your brother and his wife seem to have kept themselves to themselves.'

'But surely there will need to be witnesses to prove her defence, too?' Joe asked.

'Presumably. We're doing all we can to investigate exactly what happened and what kind of relationship they had. The information you gave me about your brother's attempt on your life will, of course, be integral to the case, and in due course you'll most likely be called to give evidence to the events of that time.'

'What? But what has that all got to do with Pam killing him? Surely I don't have to be involved?' Joe was horrified. He hadn't expected this, and to have to go over everything in court was the last thing he wanted. It also occurred to him that if he testified to David running him down, it would only strengthen Pam's claim that he was a violent man. What had he got himself into?

'I'm sorry, Mr Parker, but depending on what charge the CPS pursue, it's a very likely possibility that you will be called to give evidence. Now, I have the address and number of the landlord of the flat your brother rented. He's aware that you're here this weekend and that you need to see the flat.'

Joe took the piece of paper Armstrong offered and left the police station in a daze. Having assumed that telling the detective the truth and holding nothing back was the best way forward, now it seemed as if his honesty would assist Pam in getting away with murder, quite literally.

Joe sat in his car, trying to get his head round what had happened and also what might be in store for him in the near future. He didn't want to get involved with any part of David's life, but now it seemed as if he was the one left to sort out the mess his brother had left behind.

Eventually he pulled out his phone and dialled the number which Armstrong had given him. He spoke briefly to his brother's landlord and agreed to meet him at the flat later that afternoon. Joe's next task was to pick up a death certificate from the hospital and register the death at the registrar's office. Mentally, he thanked Phil for the crash course he'd received in the red tape involved after a death. Wading through the bureaucracy after Alison's death had been difficult and he'd certainly not expected to be repeating the process so soon afterwards.

George Thompson could have been anywhere between sixty and seventy years old, Joe found it difficult to tell. He was a short, stocky man with a head far too large for his body, a ruddy complexion, a large, bulbous nose and he reeked of cigarettes and beer. Thompson was inside the flat when Joe arrived and was obviously not in the best of humour.

'I need this place clearing out, and fast!' was his greeting. 'The police have kept me out too bloody long and I'm losing money on it, and mentioning money, your brother owed seven hundred pounds in rent and I don't take cheques or cards.'

'Seven hundred? I don't carry that much round with me in cash.' Joe was taken aback. It seemed that he'd not only have to pay for a funeral, but settle David's debts, too.

'There's a cash machine round the corner. If you're staying here this afternoon I can call back in a couple of hours to collect it.'

'I bet you can!'

'Look, you're getting off bloody lightly with only seven hundred quid. They haven't exactly looked after this place as you can see, and I'll have work to do before I can let it again. Be grateful I'm not asking for more. And now it's got the stigma of having a murder committed here an' all. Who's going to want to live here now, eh?'

Thompson was a real bundle of joy, Joe thought. 'I'll get your money if you'll leave me a key. Two hours is all I need so if you're back then it'll be waiting for you and you can have the key back.'

'When're you gonna move the stuff out then?'

'I doubt I'll want to take anything so I'll put it in the hands of a house clearer. Can I give them your name and number to liaise with?' This seemed to be the most sensible thing to do. Joe already wanted to be out of this flat, it reeked of misery, and his eyes kept straying to a dark patch on the worn, dirty carpet which he felt sure was his brother's blood.

'Okay by me, as long as they can do it quickly.' Thompson left a key and said he'd be back in two hours' time.

Joe looked around, appalled that his brother had come to this; the flat was small, yes, but the state of it horrified him. He thought about his parents and the way they had brought up the two brothers. They too had had very little money and lived in a small rented house, with second-hand furniture and very little in the way of luxuries, but the house was always spotless, the floors scrubbed and everything neat and tidy.

His mother would have been shocked to see the filth her eldest son had ended his days in. Unwashed pots filled the kitchen sink, a pedal bin overflowed with rubbish, the odour of rotting food filling the room. Joe understood that the police had been working at the flat as a crime scene, but this was more than a couple of weeks' worth of neglect.

Sickened by his surroundings, Joe decided to walk to the cash point and fill his lungs with fresh air before facing the task of looking through his brother's meagre possessions.

Two hours later, Joe was more than ready to leave. The police had initially taken David's suitcase away but it had been returned to the flat and seeing it in the hallway, Joe felt a cursory look inside was necessary. It certainly wasn't packed neatly, either David packed in a hurry or the police had found nothing of interest and didn't bother to leave the contents in any kind of order.

It contained everything necessary for several days, or even weeks away, but the item that surprised Joe the most was a letter addressed to him, already stamped and ready to post. It had been hidden deep in a side pocket, which may have been why the police hadn't taken it as evidence. He took the letter over to the window where he perched, wearily, on the arm of a chair and opened it with apprehension. It was in his brother's handwriting, still familiar to Joe from their shared childhood and still able to tug at his emotions. Tears blurred his vision as he unfolded the paper and began to read.

My Dear Joe

I am consumed with guilt and I have no expectations of your forgiveness, or compassion, but I'm going away and I wanted to try to make you understand how I reached such deplorable depths.

We were never close as boys and with hindsight I now know that it was my fault and I allowed jealousy to make me such an awful brother. Sadly, we can never go back and live our past again any more than we can predict our future, but I'm going to try for a new start. When I'm settled and back on my feet, I'll get in touch, but for the moment I don't want you to know where I'm going, so you won't think I'm asking for charity.

It would be easy to pass all the blame on to Pamela for what happened but at the end of the day it was me driving the car and I have to take responsibility for that. You never really knew my wife, and I'm hoping that knowing some of my struggles with her will help you to understand why I behaved so badly. Life wasn't always unkind to us and our marriage was punctuated with fluctuating fortunes. For several years, we lived in comfort in an exclusive apartment with a sea view in Bournemouth. I held down a reasonably good job as a sales rep, with generous commission topping up my salary, a company car and other perks which we enjoyed, yet took for granted.

When the economy slowed and the company began to squeeze employees to produce more sales for less reward, I stood my ground, demanding to have my salary reinstated; such was my inflated opinion of my worth. Pam encouraged me in this but my insistence only resulted in being fired on the spot. I'd stupidly played into their hands, idiot that I am. Pam sympathised for a while, massaging my wounded ego, until the weeks turned into months and no new job was forthcoming. She then began to nag, grumbling about the lack of money for the luxuries she'd come to expect in life and goading me for being an inadequate provider. When she eventually found out that I'd stopped paying the rent on the apartment and gambled away our meagre savings, she took control of the finances and we were forced to leave the expensive area of Bournemouth and move to Eastleigh.

The move was imperative due to the increasingly frequent visits by heavies from the loan company I'd unwisely borrowed from, and the fact that the landlord was threatening eviction for non-payment of rent. It was what our mother would have called a 'moonlight flit' and in reality our new address was in fact a hiding place. The living conditions were far from desirable, but they were safe, even though we'd been unable to bring with us anything which did not fit into the car. We were living in a rented shoebox of a flat, with windows which didn't close properly, damp in all the rooms and yellowing wallpaper. The close proximity of the railway lines ensured our sleep was regularly broken, and our relationship was becoming strained. We constantly snapped at each other over the slightest little thing.

We convinced ourselves this was just a temporary blip in our circumstances and things would improve soon, as they had in the past, but we were wrong. After three years of living hand to mouth, we were both angry at the world for the way we perceived we'd been treated, yet neither of us was prepared to take any kind of job which we considered beneath us as a way to alleviate our circumstances. Instead, I'm ashamed to say that I feigned a back injury in order to claim benefits and Pam took to shoplifting to provide her with the luxuries she coveted and which she convinced herself were necessary for her happiness. Still it was not enough and we were forever looking for the golden opportunity which we felt one day would come our way.

Oh Joe, how low we had sunk, love and respect for each other had long disappeared and I was beginning to loath Pam almost as much as I loathed myself.

When we received your letter telling us that Alison had died in an accident, I was devastated for you but then Pam began to work on me. She thought this could be our chance to improve our lot in life. She convinced me that you would be compensated from the accident and would probably gain from Alison's life insurance. Pam's permanently sour expression lifted and her features became quite animated as she snatched the letter from me to read for herself. Sadly, that was probably the moment the 'plan' began to form, and that's when we decided to attend the funeral.

After that debacle I felt such shame at how crass and insensitive we'd been but Pam was fuelled with anger and couldn't settle, determined to come out on top, at any cost. It was just silly talk at first, drunken ramblings, I didn't think she was seriously considering murder. However, Pam persuaded me to go along with it, not simply with her talk of your money and home but with her usual goading and belittling me. I should never have listened to her but I was so low and rose to her challenges to 'be a man for once', and so I did it, or so I thought.

Driving back to Eastleigh, I felt a sense of complete self-disgust and deep regret at what I'd just done. I had murdered my only brother.

Things happened swiftly after that and my hatred of Pam was building inside, a cancer eating into me. The only relief I found was when we came back to Greater Manchester and discovered that you were alive. Conflicting emotions battled inside of me but the primary one was of relief. That's what's given me the hope that I might be able to turn my life *around, so I'm leaving Pam, on the quiet of course. She would never willingly let me go. I'm just waiting for my opportunity, when she'll be out of the house for long enough to allow for my escape.*

And so, Joe, I don't know what you'll think of this letter, an excuse, an explanation or just the ramblings of a bloody fool? Whatever you think, I hope that someday we will meet again and begin to heal our traumatised souls together. But whatever happens, I am so, so sorry.

Your penitent brother,

David

Joe was exhausted by the time he finished the letter. His emotions were still conflicted but if anything, it made him long even more for his brother to still be alive so that they could talk things through properly and start again. But it was too late, Pam had had the last word on David's future. He'd failed in his attempt to escape from her.

Joe pocketed the letter and then searched everywhere else he thought there might be important documents, but found very little. Two out-of-date passports, a couple of empty cheque books, several old bank statements, and a post office savings account from thirty years ago with less than five pounds in it, was the extent of his findings.

He put them all in a plastic carrier bag to take home for shredding, then found a roll of bin liners and threw in the worst of the rubbish lying around the flat. He filled a dustbin at the back of the building and left several bags beside it, hoping the rubbish would be collected soon.

After paying George Thompson off, Joe couldn't wait to get away and drove back to the Premier Inn where he ordered a large whisky in the bar.

He hadn't realised how extreme his brother's circumstances had become, but if he had, would he have behaved any differently, could he have done anything about it? Joe would never know; it was too late now, and David was dead. He would arrange the funeral in due course as, like in Alison's case, an inquest was to be held, meaning a delay in the body being released. It seemed that this and paying off his debts, was all that Joe could do for his only brother.

CHAPTER 27

Hannah followed the progress of Timmy's Farm with interest, often turning to the Facebook page to read the regular updates. Now that her memory had returned, there'd been no doubt that she would attend their open day; she was far more confident and actually looked forward to meeting the Joneses.

Mel and Sam were keen to attend too, which delighted her, as she was only too aware that they would both be leaving for university in just a few more weeks, so any time spent with them was precious.

The night before the open day Hannah's leg had been playing up. Phantom pains woke her through the night and she'd risen several times to walk around in an effort to ease the surreal feeling, eventually taking a tablet in the hope of sleep. The morning found her tired but still keen to visit Timmy's farm and hopefully meet Alan and Cassie Jones, a couple who were elevated to the status of heroes to her mind.

On their arrival, Hannah was delighted to find parking reserved for disabled drivers which significantly cut down on the distance she would need to walk. The mood was decidedly festive, with bunting fluttering in the breeze and the unusually bright September sun bathing the whole scene with kaleidoscopic prisms of light. A party atmosphere buoyed the general mood and children's laughter could be heard from every corner of the farm.

The whole area was incredibly busy. Both Hannah and her children happily dropped donations into the buckets and then moved on to learn more about this remarkable project, which touched them perhaps more than most, feeling something of a connection to the Joneses' loss.

Mel saw Hannah looking at a couple with a new born baby and she squeezed her mother's hand. Hannah knew that Mike and Sarah had had their baby, but she wasn't ready yet to meet the child, as that would obviously mean meeting Sarah too. The divorce was, however, almost finalised and thankfully it had been amicable, as she'd wished.

Mel and Sam had been to visit Mike and Sarah in their new home and Mel had tentatively told Hannah all about her new sister. Hannah pleased that Mike's relationship with the twins seemed better than ever and happy to see Mel taking so much pleasure in her half-sibling.

Sam picked up a leaflet with information on the farm and a layout diagram, and proceeded to steer his mother and sister in the direction of the animals. Volunteers were at hand to answer questions and tell the stories of some of the farm's residents, many of which were quite harrowing, but due to the work of the farm, now had a happy ending.

Hannah was impressed with the tremendous effort the Joneses had so obviously put into making their son's dream a reality. There were a couple of buildings where visitors were not allowed, one a hospital block and the other a quiet space for new or timid animals to settle in. But there were photographs outside these areas, showing the interior and some of the occupants, images which elicited many oohs and ahs from the visitors.

Other than these restricted areas there was so much to see. Donkeys, Shetland ponies and goats were enjoying the attentions of the visitors and probably being given far too much food, while cats weaved in and out of the multitude of legs as if they owned the place, which in a way, of course, they did.

After an hour or so, Hannah needed to sit down, so they made their way towards a marquee which sold refreshments for a welcome cup of tea and a break. Sam went to fetch the drinks while Mel stayed with Hannah. There was obviously something Mel wanted to say and Hannah eventually said, 'Come on then, spit it out.'

'Oh, Mum, you just seem so sad at times and I worry about you…'

'Now, you can stop all that. I'm doing really well, thank you.' Hannah forced a smile — this visit had been a good idea, she was almost telling the truth.

'I saw the way you looked at those animals and all the children playing with them,' Mel continued, 'it made me think of baby Charlotte and then I felt guilty. You must feel awful, and I'm not sure if it upsets you if I mention her?'

'Don't ever think that. It's only right that you should have a relationship with Charlotte … and your dad. Please stop worrying about me, I think the time's fast approaching when I should meet her, too. My son and daughter can't have a little sister whom I've never met, can they?'

'Oh, Mum, do you mean that? You should see her, she's a sweetheart and I love the way she curls her chubby little fingers around mine. And Dad's changed too, he really has. I'm not saying that what he did was right but he regrets all the hurt he's caused and he'd be thrilled if you'd visit Charlotte. He always asks after you. He still cares for us all, Mum.'

Hannah knew that her daughter lived in a world where she wanted everything to be perfect, everyone to be friends and the sun to shine every day. She hoped Mel's life would prove to be such, and for now Hannah would happily do all she could to keep this idyll a reality for as long as possible.

'Mel, I understand why your dad left. I was angry at the time but I'm over that now. We've spoken on the phone occasionally and we'll always be connected through you and Sam. I might even take a leaf out of his book and go a bit wild myself.' Hannah was pleased to see her daughter smile.

'You're the best, Mum, a real superhero, and I love you.'

'I love you too — you and Sam are the best thing that ever happened to me.'

Sam returned with the cups of tea and it was then that Hannah saw Cassie Jones. The woman was heading her way and Hannah was unsure whether she wanted to speak with her or not, but then she reminded herself that there was absolutely no reason why she shouldn't, and she deserved being congratulated on such a remarkable achievement.

Cassie smiled as she neared Hannah's table, and Hannah reached up to catch her arm.

'Mrs Jones?' she said. Cassie sat down on a seat next to her and smiled. 'My name's Hannah Graham. I'd just like to say how wonderful this is, it's remarkable, and you've done such an amazing job.'

'Thank you, Mrs Graham. I remember you from the inquest. How are you doing?'

'I'm fine, thank you, up and about again now.' She gave a rather embarrassed smile.

'So I see. I'm really pleased for you, and thank you for coming today. We all lost so much that awful day, and it's good to catch up on how others are getting along. I've just been talking to Joe Parker; I don't know if you remember him, he lost his wife in the accident?'

'Oh yes, I bumped into Joe at the hospital. How is he?'

'Well, he seems to be heading your way, so perhaps he can tell you for himself?' Cassie smiled as she nodded towards where Joe was approaching, and then she stood up to leave her seat free. 'It's been lovely to meet you, Mrs Graham, please keep in touch; it would be good to chat when I've more time.' With that she left and a smiling Joe Parker slid into her seat.

'I thought it was you!' He sounded really pleased to see her and Hannah introduced him to her children.

'Isn't this wonderful, Alan and Cassie have worked tremendously hard to achieve all this.' Joe was obviously impressed.

'They certainly have,' Hannah agreed. 'And this weather's perfect. Who would have thought we could have one of the best summers for years after such an abysmal winter?'

They were both thoughtful for a moment, silently remembering exactly what the winter had cost them.

Sam broke into the silence. 'Mum, will you be okay if we go and explore a bit more? Mel wants to get a few more pictures.'

'Of course, take your time, love; I'll probably still be here, drinking the teapot dry.'

Sam and Mel said goodbye to Joe and left to see the rest of the farm.

'Your daughter's the image of you, you must be very proud of them,' Joe remarked.

'I am, they're great kids, both off to uni soon so I'll miss them like crazy, but don't tell them I said so!'

'Your secret's safe with me!'

'So, how are you getting on, Joe?'

'Okay — well ... maybe not okay, you know?'

Hannah nodded.

'I almost envy Cassie and Alan for the way they've channelled their grief into something so positive,' Joe continued. 'They're an extraordinary couple and what they've done here is nothing short of amazing. I didn't know them before so I never met Timmy, but he must have been a remarkable young man to inspire all this. They seem to have found a reason to keep going, to cope with their grief; I suppose that's what I envy...' Joe looked as if his thoughts were miles away. 'They say we all find our own coping mechanisms, eventually.'

'So how do you cope?' Hannah looked directly into his eyes.

'Nothing so original for me, I'm afraid, simply taking one day at a time. They say time heals but just lately time seems to bring one problem after another. My brother died a couple of months ago too. He was murdered.'

As Hannah listened she studied the man sitting just a few feet away from her. He had the air of having lived through so much and a depth of experience was etched in his face, lines of sadness and loss covered what must once have been laughter lines, and grief was evident in his eyes. She hoped that for Joe there could still be joy, dreams and possibilities. He deserved no less. Empathy flooded through her as he shared with her the recent events in his life.

'Oh, that's terrible for you, I'm so sorry! You must be devastated?'

'Well, I can't claim that we were close and it's a bit of a long story, I wouldn't want to bore you with all the details...'

'It wouldn't bore me at all and I've been told I'm a pretty good listener.'

'Another time perhaps?'

'Yes, another time.' Hannah smiled.

'How about you, Hannah, how are you managing?'

'Rather like you I suppose, a day at a time. As you see I'm upright again and have become quite a whiz on crutches when the leg gets too much.'

'Good for you, it can't be easy. Is your husband not with you today?' Joe looked around.

'Ah, that's another story, we've split up.'

'Oh, Hannah, I'm sorry, and here's me going on about my woes!'

'Don't worry, at least he hasn't died.'

'It wasn't because of the accident was it, your leg, I mean?'

'No, apparently there was someone else, a younger woman and they've recently had a baby. As always I was the last to know, or even suspect.' Hannah's empty laugh at her own words didn't hide the hurt that was evident in her eyes.

'That must be difficult. Can I be so presumptuous as to go on record as saying he must be a total fool?' Joe looked earnestly at Hannah and her eyes began to fill with tears. 'Now I've upset you, sorry again! Can I get you another cup of tea? I think I'd like one now.'

'Good idea.' Hannah sniffed.

As Joe left her for a few moments, she blew her nose and took a few deep breaths. Perhaps they should stick to talking about the weather, it was much safer, but she liked Joe, he'd been through so much and it appeared to give them a bond. Hannah wondered if there really would be 'another time' and found herself hoping that there would.

CHAPTER 28

Joe had begun to notice an improvement in his general health of late which he had no hesitation in attributing to giving up smoking. It hadn't been an easy journey, but it was now over four months since he'd smoked his last cigarette. He'd lost weight too, not consciously and not perhaps in the best of ways, sometimes it was simply because he forgot to eat, but he felt better for it and knew that Alison would be proud of him.

Attending a social event without Alison still felt strange to Joe, but the project at Timmy's Farm was so fascinating that he soon became absorbed in all that was going on around him. Meeting Hannah Graham again was an unexpected pleasure too; she was so easy to talk to, straightforward and honest, qualities which he'd always admired in a person. They talked in a general manner, both in awe of the Joneses' hard work, and on a deeper level too, as Joe shared some of the details of his brother's death, and Hannah told him that she and her husband were now separated.

She also shared the better news that she'd regained her memories of the accident, and it was so obvious to Joe that a weight had been lifted from her by the realisation that she hadn't been to blame. Joe assured her again, as he had at the hospital, of his certainty that there'd been nothing that she or anyone else could have done that day. Still, he could understand her relief and he would probably have felt much the same himself in Hannah's situation.

Joe really wanted to see her again and was pretty sure that she felt the same, yet he'd been embarrassed about asking for her phone number, feeling like a tongue-tied schoolboy. Their shared life-changing experience of the accident seemed to have created a bond between them, and now that they were both on their own, why shouldn't they meet up as friends? He hoped that perhaps Hannah would like to go out to dinner with him one night; he missed such simple pleasures and thought that she probably did too. With the certainty that she was honest enough to say no if the idea didn't appeal to her, he could only ask, but he rather hoped she would say yes.

The open day helped to fill in the weekend, pleasantly so, and Joe returned to work on Monday morning ready to focus on the growing pile of accounts on his desk. Before he made any great inroads into the day's work, however, he was disturbed by a telephone call from DS Armstrong. Joe's heart sank; he hadn't heard from the detective for several weeks and assumed that no news was good news, so what did the man want now?

'Good morning, Mr Parker. I need to update you on Mrs Pamela Parker's circumstances.' As ever, Armstrong's speech sounded as if it was straight from a textbook. 'After an incident at the women's facility where she is being held, it has been necessary to move her to a secure psychiatric hospital.'

'And can you tell me what this incident was?' Joe asked.

'The latest one, and there have been a few minor incidents of a similar ilk, was an attack on another detainee. Mrs Parker appears to have lost control and attacked this other woman quite ferociously, leaving her with serious injuries.'

Joe's heart sank. 'So how does this affect the trial? Will it still go ahead as planned?' He'd been dreading the trial and giving evidence, evidence which he knew might actually support Pam's claims that David had been an abusive husband.?

'Ah, well.' DS Armstrong cleared his throat. 'It now appears that Mrs Armstrong may not be standing trial. Her solicitor has put forward a motion to have the charges dismissed due to her precarious mental health.'

'And will that happen?'

'It's too early to say, but the judge has ordered a round of psychiatric evaluations and these things take time. The CPS still wishes to proceed with the charges, but of course the tests will have to be completed before any decision is made.'

'So if the trial doesn't go ahead will she just get away with it?' Joe was horrified to think that David's death might go unpunished.

'I wouldn't put it quite like that. If she is declared unfit to stand trial, at the very least she'll be committed to some sort of psychiatric institution for treatment. I will keep you informed of any further developments and of course if I can help in any other way, please give me a call.'

After work, when Joe picked Liffey up from Phil and Helen's, he shared with them what the detective had told him that morning.

'My goodness me, she must be absolutely mad,' Helen said, her husband nodding in agreement.

'So will the trial be delayed?' Phil asked.

'It could even be cancelled,' Joe told them. 'DS Armstrong said that her solicitor is asking for the charges to be dismissed due to her failing mental health. I don't know what to think to be quite honest. I was dreading the trial, but the thought of Pam getting away with his murder is too shocking to even contemplate. I don't know what's going to happen now, but it's obviously going to drag on and on. These evaluations take time apparently. At the back of my mind is the thought that Pam could be faking this mental illness to avoid standing trial. What do you think?'

'Oh, Joe, we don't know her well enough to make that kind of judgement, but if she is faking it I shouldn't think years in a mental institution will be a much better option than prison. And if she's proving to be violent, she'll be kept in some kind of secure facility surely, and who would want that for goodness knows how many years?' Helen asked.

'Perhaps you're right. She's going to be locked away whatever happens. I'll just have to be patient and wait to see what these evaluations throw up.'

Joe took Liffey down to the meadow before going home to feed her. The weather was still holding and the earth was bone dry, the grass scorched and bleached of its usual cool green colour. He thought about the year behind him, the ferocious arctic weather which caused that fateful accident and changed so many lives; a cruel, indiscriminate ripple effect, stealing life, happiness and health from all of those involved. And the contrast now, from such fierce winter weather to one of the hottest summers he could remember, was incredible.

David came into his mind too, and the pain he'd added to Joe's already broken world, but he was still his brother and Joe would never have wished him dead. He had decided not to share David's letter with DS Armstrong. It seemed unnecessary now that Pamela looked unlikely to be standing trial, and Joe had decided the letter was something he wanted to cherish privately and keep to himself.

Sighing, Joe turned his face to the summer sun. How would the latter part of the year unfold? Surely, Joe thought, he'd been allotted more than his share of misery. Could there possibly be something good waiting for him around the corner?

CHAPTER 29

Rosie wanted to hear all about Timmy's Farm; she'd been disappointed at not being able to go to the open day, but work had taken priority. They were sitting in Hannah's lounge enjoying a glass of wine and the peace and quiet of a Sunday afternoon. Hannah had taken her prosthesis off and swung her leg up onto the sofa, as she'd been cleaning all morning and now it was playing up. Rosie was probably one of the few people she felt comfortable enough with to do this.

'It's amazing, Rosie, they must have worked so hard to achieve all that in just a few months. Of course, their farm lends itself perfectly to such a project, the space is ideal and they've utilised all the outbuildings, it's incredible. I had a brief chat to Cassie, but obviously she was busy — everyone wanted to congratulate her. I'd thought about volunteering in some way but honestly, what could I do with this leg?'

'There's plenty you could do! It won't be all mucking out and grooming ponies you know, there's bound to be paperwork, and your organisational skills are second to none. Give her a ring, or send an email — you might be exactly what they're looking for.'

'Do you think so? It's just that when the twins go to uni it's going to be so quiet around here. I don't want to give myself time to sit and mope, and it's such a worthwhile venture.' Hannah was really dreading the day Mel and Sam would leave, a day which was drawing closer. It would have been bad enough if Mike was still with her but being alone was a scary prospect.

'Well, you won't know unless you ask,' Rosie encouraged her. 'Did the twins enjoy it?'

'Oh yes, they were most impressed, everyone was. You know, I really couldn't have gone if I hadn't remembered the details of the accident. I'd been carrying around that awful dread that I'd somehow been to blame for the whole thing and it was getting to me.'

'So they didn't treat you like some kind of social pariah then?' Rosie smiled, playfully mocking her friend.

'No, not at all, I felt quite relaxed with Cassie, and I met Joe Parker in the tea tent too. I needed a sit down and the twins left me there for a while. We had quite a long chat. I suppose I feel more self-assured now that I know the whole thing wasn't my fault, I'm a victim of a freak accident just the same as they are.'

'Joe Parker? Isn't he the one whose wife died in the accident?'

'Yes, that's right. We met briefly at the hospital when I went for my first fitting and I was glad of the opportunity to thank him for his testimony at the inquest, so it was good to see him again. His brother's died since the accident too; it must be awful for him.'

'Bloody hell! That seems a bit unfair.' Rosie's face suddenly split into a huge grin as she asked, 'So what's he like, this Joe?'

'Oh, Rosie, don't think that, he's just a nice man who I shared a cup of tea with.'

'Well, why shouldn't I think like that? You're single, he's single and you're a very attractive woman, Hannah Graham. Is he, you know, fit?'

'He's just a lovely man who I met by chance. He's just lost his wife, for heaven's sake, and besides, he'd never be interested in me!'

'Why ever not?'

'You know why not.' Hannah absently rubbed her leg. 'It's repulsive.' There, she'd said it; she was convinced that no man would consider her to be attractive, ever again.

'So you're an expert now on what repulses this Joe, are you?'

'Any man would be repulsed by it ... this stump, it's ugly, hideous...'

'Hannah, listen to me. Your stump does not define you! You are still the same person you were before this accident — a warm, caring person and, hell woman, look in the mirror, you're gorgeous. Besides, from what you tell me, Joe sounds a very nice person but if having a prosthetic leg puts him off, then he's not worth having. You'd have to give him, or any man for that matter, a chance to prove that he's not that shallow.'

Hannah suddenly burst into tears and Rosie moved beside her to wrap a comforting arm around her shoulder.

'Go on then, let it all out,' Rosie whispered as Hannah released all her pent-up emotions in huge sobs.

After a few minutes Hannah quietened and began to apologise. 'I'm sorry, Rosie; I really thought I was done with all the tears, the feeling sorry for myself.'

'Don't apologise, tears are cathartic and you bottle things up far too much. A good cry does us all good sometimes. You don't always have to be brave, Hannah; none of us can be strong all the time and you've had a lot going on recently.'

'Thanks, Rosie, maybe you're right. It's been all losses this year, first my leg, then Mike and now the twins. I know all children have to grow up and leave home, but I'm not looking forward to it. The house will be so quiet.'

'I'll do my best to make more noise, shall I?' Rosie asked. They laughed together and Rosie refilled their wine glasses.

'Getting back to this Joe, did you give him your telephone number?'

'Well, actually, I did. We do seem to hit it off well and I think we could get along, as friends, so when he asked if I'd mind if he rang me sometime, just to see how I was getting on, I said that would be fine.' Hannah could feel herself blushing.

'Good for you, it sounds as if you could both do with some company. You might be good for each other.'

When Rosie left, Hannah's mood switched once again and she became reflective. The twins wouldn't be in for another couple of hours but she shouldn't rely on them for company. She was proud of them both, Sam was to study sports science at university and Mel had chosen journalism and media studies. They would do well, and Hannah knew that wasn't just her biased opinion.

Over the last few months Sam had changed the most, his frame had at last filled out, probably with all the extra sports he was doing, and his confidence had grown too. Working at the sports centre gave him the opportunity to meet so many new people and his social circle increased almost overnight. He was protective towards his mother though, demonstrating a gentle side which Mike always said came from her. Mel had been writing articles covering a wide range of topics and submitting them to magazines for publication. Several had been accepted and Hannah was so proud to see Mel's name in print beneath an article she had written. Mel had even taken her camera and notebook to Timmy's Farm the previous day, and with permission from Alan Jones, made notes for a feature on the project. Hannah knew she didn't need to worry about her children, but she would miss them so much. Perhaps Rosie was right and she needed to work on increasing her own social circle.

CHAPTER 30

David's funeral was the saddest one Joe had ever attended, not for the expected reasons, but because he and the undertaker were the only ones present. It was such a contrast to the packed service for Alison, when people Joe didn't even know had turned up to pay their respects.

David had not been religious, and so a civil celebrant presided over a very short service at the Eastleigh crematorium, and when the curtains closed it seemed as if David's life was not just over but would be forgotten by everyone, except his brother. But what would Joe's memories of him be? Sadly perhaps, the most abiding one would be of the day he tried to kill him. Seeing David's face at the wheel of the car was an image which would never leave Joe, but above all else, he was saddened that his brother's life had been ended in such a violent way. It would probably be months before Pam's trial and he'd heard nothing new from DS Armstrong which presumably meant that nothing was happening.

Joe was glad to get home, and the welcome he received from Liffey went a long way to bringing him comfort. He had good friends, a lovely home and even though he still missed Alison with every fibre of his being, he was learning to be grateful for what he did have.

Thoughts of his wife prompted thoughts of her mother. It was over a month since he'd spoken to Ethel on the phone, a conversation which was brief, as someone knocked on her door only a minute after she answered the phone. The old lady hadn't rung back, so Joe assumed she didn't want to talk, but for Alison's sake he felt he should visit her again to make sure she was coping okay.

It was a duty visit which he embarked upon one Saturday morning, without forewarning her to let her know that he was coming.

Joe rang the doorbell and almost immediately heard her voice through the entry intercom. When she buzzed him in and he stood before her in the lounge, she looked him up and down.

'Well, it is you, I thought you were dead, too!' Ethel's tone was, as always, sarcastic.

Why does she always have to be so bloody snarky, he thought but pressed his lips tightly together to stop himself replying in a similar fashion. After a moment he said, 'I've been in an accident, Ethel, and I've been laid up for a while.' For some reason he didn't want to tell her about David's death; it was still very raw and Ethel was the last person he wanted asking intrusive questions and prying into his affairs.

Ethel squinted at him. 'Huh, another accident, that's a bit careless, isn't it?'

'I'm getting better now, thank you!' Joe replied. 'Anyway, how are you? Did you get any help from Social Services sorted out?'

'Don't talk to me about Social Services, they're useless. A lady came to visit and just about gave me the third degree. If I want any help I have to tell them everything; they even want to assess my finances and expect me to tell them every penny I have. Then there'll be another visit to assess my care needs! And even after jumping through all of their hoops they want me to pay for the service, it's ridiculous!'

It was no more than Joe had expected but he didn't offer an opinion. 'So what have you decided to do?' he asked instead.

'Well, Mrs Hoskins in the bungalow across the street suggested I put an ad in the newsagent's window, so I did. A nice young girl came round, Christina her name is, from Romania or some such place, and she started almost straight away.'

'And is she good, are you happy with her?' Now that he was more relaxed and looked around the flat, it did look clean and tidy.

'Oh yes, she'll do anything; shopping, cleaning, laundry and cooking, and she's a lot cheaper than Social Services were going to be!'

'That's good, I'm glad you're sorted out.' Joe was relieved that help was in place for her, if only for Alison's sake.

'It's no thanks to you, though, is it? I could have starved to death for all you care.'

She had to go and spoil it, to have another dig at him. *Well two can play at that game*, Joe thought. 'Ethel, you're far more able than you make out, if only you'd get up off your backside and do things for yourself occasionally, you'd probably feel much better!'

'How dare you talk to me like that!'

'It's time someone did! You think the world revolves around you, but here's the news, it doesn't! And while we're having this little heart to heart, I'd like to point out that you maligned the memory of your daughter by your vicious lies. I've found out the truth about the baby, and you don't come out of that situation too well either.'

'Don't blame me! She got herself pregnant; she had to suffer the consequences.'

'No, Ethel, your daughter was raped and she was only eighteen! Don't you have any compassion in that cold heart of yours? It wasn't Alison's fault at all, she was abused and suffered greatly for it, and you have the gall to throw it at me, telling me only half the story and besmirching her memory in the process? And I'm sure she got very little comfort from you at the time. Aren't you ashamed of yourself?'

Ethel's mouth was open; she'd probably never been spoken to like that before, and if Joe hadn't been so angry he would have laughed at her horrified expression. Had he gone too far, he wondered? No, perhaps he should have said this years ago, and if he'd known about Alison's past he probably would have too.

'I think I'd like you to leave now!' Ethel's chin was high and she couldn't look her son-in-law in the eye.

'Yes, I think that's a very good idea, but if ever you feel like apologising you've got my number.'

'Me, apologise! It's you who should be doing that. I'm an old woman and I'm ill, how dare you treat me like this?' She glared at him now, recovering from the shock of Joe's pertinent words.

'You're as ill as it suits, you don't fool me, and you didn't fool Alison either! She knew what you were really like but she cared for you out of duty, because she was that kind of person. You don't know how lucky you were to have had a daughter like her!' Perhaps he'd said too much. 'Yes, I'll go now but I hope you have the decency to think about what I've said.'

With those words Joe turned and walked out of the door, quite sure he would never hear from Ethel again.

CHAPTER 31

September made way for October with Hannah welcoming the signs of autumn as a break from the hot, dry summer. Hannah couldn't remember there ever being such a contrast between the awful winter weather they'd experienced, followed by such a scorching summer. There was much talk about global warming and whether they could expect such extremes of weather as the norm from now on. But it wasn't only the end of summer which sat heavily on Hannah's heart; it was her children leaving for university.

Mel was preparing to go to Cardiff University. She'd been so excited when her grades matched what she needed to take up their offer and couldn't wait to begin the course. The university had a reputation for excellence in her chosen field and was her natural first choice. Over the holidays she'd been delighted to have even more success selling articles to magazines and Hannah was particularly proud of the feature she'd written on Cassie and Alan's venture of Timmy's Farm.

Cassie and Alan had agreed to be interviewed by Mel and the resulting article was an empathic, human interest story of which Hannah was so proud. Her daughter would be the first to leave home, her bags were packed and Hannah was driving her to Cardiff the next day. Sam would leave two days later for Swansea.

In Hannah's ideal world, her children would have found places at the same university, but as their chosen courses were so different, this hadn't been an option. They would, however, be geographically close enough to meet up on occasions and even travel home together for weekends and holidays, a thought which Hannah contented herself with.

Mike had offered to take Sam to Swansea and Hannah had agreed; he was Mike's son too and the children were seeing quite a bit of him and Sarah at the moment, mainly due to them both being captivated by baby Charlotte.

The twins had celebrated their eighteenth birthdays at the end of August. Neither wanted extravagant parties for which Hannah was silently thankful, and instead, Sam asked for a new laptop and Mel an iPhone. Both of them appeared to be happy; they had overcome the effects of the accident and also, it seemed, the divorce for which Hannah was relieved. They were on the threshold of their own journeys in life and she hoped and prayed that they would continue to make the right choices for their own future happiness.

Hannah often reflected on the changes the year had presented. The negative ones were becoming easier to live with and she stubbornly determined to maintain a pragmatic view on life. She supposed the grieving process for her lost leg was gradually turning into acceptance; it would never be easy to live with, and there were days where she suffered considerable pain, but she accepted it as something which could never be changed.

The shock of losing Mike hurt deeply, although she often thought she should have seen it coming. The fact that he'd been having an affair for so long was a bitter blow, humiliating as well as hurtful, but looking back, it was clear that her marriage was never going to survive. She and Mike had grown too far apart and left it too long before either of them admitted to any problems. Hannah truly wished him well and was pleased that he seemed so happy with his new family. He would always be her children's father, a fact which would connect them forever, and who knows, in time she might even feel brave enough to meet Sarah.

And now that the twins were leaving home, Hannah faced another huge change, but not everything which was happening in her life was negative. She'd begun to work a couple of evenings a week with Cassie and Alan Jones and they had called her a godsend for how well she had organised their office. The couple were so busy caring for their animals, marketing and fundraising, that much of the everyday paperwork had been in a mess.

Hannah's skills in organisation soon had a massive effect. She introduced systems for payment of bills, ordering of feed and other essential stock, and generally kept the office running smoothly, much to the delight of Cassie and Alan, and the three were quickly becoming firm friends.

It was Hannah's intention to work the occasional Saturday morning once the twins left home, as it would help to fill some of her weekend and she was beginning to love being at the farm. The atmosphere was something special, they were restoring health to neglected animals and the rewards were immeasurable. Sometimes, just a little love and care brought the most remarkable returns and the animals responded with the kind of devotion which suggested that they almost knew they had been rescued and wanted to repay the kindness.

Perhaps she was getting soppy in her old age, but Hannah was moved by many of the cases they took on at the farm and now couldn't imagine her life without being part of such a wonderful venture.

Another bright spot in Hannah's life was Joe Parker. He was becoming a valued friend, someone she could talk to quite openly and she was sure he felt the same. They'd had several telephone conversations, and Joe rang most weeks just to catch up and chat about what was happening in their lives. They also exchanged occasional emails, something she enjoyed writing, particularly at night when her leg was troubling her.

Joe was always interested in the twins and in what was happening at Timmy's Farm, so she had plenty to write about and in return, he shared what was happening in his own life. It seemed to be the most natural thing in the world for them to be open and honest with each other, a fact Hannah truly appreciated; she'd had her fill of secrets and heartbreak, and wanted to carve out a different future for herself.

CHAPTER 32

The meadow was so much greener now after being parched the colour of straw during much of the long, dry summer, and it remained Liffey's favourite playground. It was November and the wind was bracing, but that didn't put either of them off and at least it was dry. During the hot weather, Liffey had splashed happily in the stream, which almost disappeared at the height of the heatwave when water became scarce, and then rolled enthusiastically in the long grass, drying off her coat and bringing a smile to Joe's face.

He enjoyed their walks together and liked to think that Alison watched down on them during their frequent forays to the meadow; she too had loved this place, especially in the early morning, and they'd so often laughed together at their dog's antics.

Joe no longer felt guilty at taking pleasure in the small things of life and a strange feeling often wrapped itself around him like a cloak, as if Ali was somehow encouraging him to live again, giving him permission to smile and laugh without that awful haunting sense of guilt hanging over him.

In the sky above, clouds swirled in a moody grey mass, but rain would be a welcome change, a blessing for the still dry earth. It was Saturday and Joe had spent more time in the meadow than usual, with nothing special to get home for, but Liffey was looking tired after bounding around chasing shadows of rabbits, so he turned to walk home.

The telephone was ringing as he unlocked the door and Joe was surprised to hear Detective Sergeant Armstrong on the line.

'Good morning, Mr Parker. I hope I'm not disturbing your Saturday?'

'Not at all. I've just come in actually — walking the dog, you know?' Joe knew the call would concern Pamela and almost dreaded what the latest development might be.

'I wanted to update you on your sister-in-law's situation. It appears that the psychiatric evaluations are now complete and the recommendation is that Pamela Parker is unfit to stand trial.'

DS Armstrong paused to let the news sink in. Joe's initial feeling was relief, as this meant he would not have to testify, but on the other hand, did it mean that Pam would get away with murdering his brother?

'So what will happen to her? Will she stand trial at a later date?' he asked.

'That seems unlikely. I've seen the medical reports. They seem to suggest that Mrs Parker's violent episodes have continued to escalate and she needs long term medication and supervision. The recommendation is treatment and detention in a secure institution. The report is quite lengthy and rather wordy as these things are, but I'm sure it could be made available to you if you wish to see it. It contains the usual jargon regarding biological and neurological reasons for her "condition", but doesn't hold out much hope of any change in the near future. As I say, my work on this case is now done and I just wanted to update you on what is, or rather, isn't, happening.'

'I don't want to see the report. There's no point in reading it as far as I can see. In a way I'm sorry that Pam won't be held accountable for her actions, but if, as it seems, she's had some kind of mental breakdown then we'll just have to accept that she'll be in the best place. At least she won't be able to harm anyone else where she is.' Joe was keen to finish the conversation and try to assimilate his thoughts on this latest development. 'Thank you for keeping me informed, DS Armstrong. I appreciate your efforts.'

The call ended and Joe smiled. *He's got me talking like a textbook now too*, he thought. He made coffee and sat in the conservatory to collect his thoughts. Perhaps this was the best outcome after all. He was fed up with all the worry and negativity of late and if this was the best he could expect, then so be it, he'd take it, and hopefully put an end to this chapter in his life.

Joe needed to tell someone and his first thought was of Hannah Graham, so he picked up the telephone and tapped in her number. Since they'd met at Timmy's Farm, he'd rung several times and they'd chatted quite easily; a comfortable bond seemed to have formed between them and it felt as if they'd known each other for years rather than just a few short months.

Joe needed to talk and he knew already that Hannah was a good listener. Perhaps he'd suggest that they go out for a meal that evening, if she was free of course. As he listened to the ringtone at the other end of the line, he found he was really looking forward to the prospect of a night out with her.

'I'd love to have dinner with you, Joe, what a lovely idea.' Hannah sounded genuinely pleased, making Joe wish he'd asked sooner. 'The twins left for university this week so a bit of cheering up is in order, thank you.'

Joe picked Hannah up later that evening and took her to a new restaurant which had been receiving rave reviews for its food. It was housed in a delightful conservatory addition to a traditional village pub, The Greyhound, and was bright and spacious with a delicious aroma wafting in from the kitchen.

They were shown to a corner table, prettily set for two, with a single rose and a lighted candle. The room was quite full but the space between the tables was generous, so they didn't feel that their conversation would be overheard. A waiter left the menus with them and they took their time over their choices.

When their food was ordered and a glass of wine poured for them both, they quite naturally fell into easy conversation. Joe remarked on how lovely Hannah looked and a blush rose to her cheeks. He then moved on to describe his conversation with DS Armstrong, while she listened intently.

'Perhaps it's for the best,' she commented when he was finished talking. 'I know how much you were dreading testifying in court, so this could be a good thing, couldn't it?'

'Yes, I suppose so, but I hate the thought that she won't stand trial and be punished for what she did.'

'She'll lose her freedom wherever she's held, and I shouldn't think a secure institute is much different from prison. Who knows, if it had gone to trial she might even have succeeded in painting David out to be the villain she said he was and got away with a more lenient sentence.'

'You're right. I need to put it behind me. There's nothing else I can do, is there? Now, tell me how it went with Mel and Sam. Are they all settled in?'

'Oh yes, and loving it by all accounts. They're both good at making friends so I know they'll be okay.'

'But you're their mother and you'll worry anyway?' Joe added, noticing the sadness creep into her eyes.

'Yes, you're right.' She smiled. 'But it's in the job description so I'm allowed!'

The conversation moved on to other topics. Hannah filled him in on her work with Cassie and Alan, and the evening passed far too quickly for them both.

Not wanting their time together to end, Hannah invited Joe in for coffee when he took her home.

'Can I help?' he asked.

'No thanks, it won't be long.' Hannah worked quickly in the kitchen, not wanting to miss a moment of Joe's company. If she'd been on her own, her prosthetic leg would have been off by now, it was uncomfortable at the end of the day, but there was no way she was going to take it off in front of Joe.

'Here we are.' She smiled as she put a full tray on the coffee table and sat next to Joe on the sofa. Their conversation flowed as before, now covering their respective plans for Christmas. Hannah would have the children home and she wondered what Joe would be doing.

'Nothing special,' was his reply. 'It'll be the first without Alison of course, and I don't think I'll feel much like celebrating.'

Hannah thought for a few moments then asked, 'Would you like to come here? It'll be strange for me too, but the twins will be home and you'll be very welcome. I'm not a bad cook either!' She gave a nervous laugh, hoping he would say yes.

'Are you sure, Hannah? I'd love to be with you, but how will the children feel about it?'

'I'm sure they'll welcome the opportunity to get to know you a little better.' They were not empty words; she knew the twins really would take to Joe.

'In that case I can hardly refuse. Thank you, I'd love to come.'

In that one evening their relationship changed and they were both aware of the subtle difference. Hannah welcomed it but was unsure how Joe was really feeling. She didn't want the evening to end but when Joe moved slowly towards her to kiss her, she felt a sudden rush of uninvited panic and pulled away.

'Joe ... doesn't this,' she put her hand on her knee, 'repulse you at all?' She had to ask; to make sure he knew what he was taking on, but as she stumbled over the words and feared what the answer might be, Joe silenced her with a kiss.

As they drew apart, the look in his eyes told her everything she needed to know. *This man will never hurt me,* she thought, *his love is solid, complete, as is mine for him!*

'Hannah,' Joe whispered, 'I think I'm falling in love with you!'

EPILOGUE

The last eighteen months had been a rollercoaster for Hannah and Joe. February's accident heralded the very worst time of their lives, a time predominantly defined by loss and fear, a terrifying event which changed everything for them, and for so many others. But then they met each other, and everything changed once again.

Joe proposed to Hannah in March, almost fourteen months since that fateful accident, and she had no hesitation in accepting. The twins were delighted for them. Sam gave Hannah away at the wedding in June, and Mel was Hannah's maid-of-honour. It was a small affair with just the twins, Hannah's neighbours Rosie and Frank, Cassie and Alan Jones, and Joe's neighbours Phil and Helen. For the reception they hired the conservatory at The Greyhound, the scene of their first date.

After the breakdown of their marriages, both out of their control, Joe and Hannah were happy to start a new life with each other, and Hannah fell in love with Liffey as soon as she met her. Joe also gained two children — something he had always longed for. They decided to move in together in a new house, to make a fresh start, and before long they were overwhelmed with joy to discover that Hannah was pregnant. Joe had assumed that he could never father children, but clearly he had been wrong, and they both felt the imminent arrival of their baby was a blessing which had been borne out of the horrific disaster that had shaped their lives all those months ago. Out of the very worst experience of Joe and Hannah's lives, beauty and joy was finally created, and they could finally put the horrors of the accident to rest.

A NOTE TO THE READER

Dear Reader,

Thank you for reading *The Accident*. The concept of ripples in a pond has always fascinated me, one action, one decision and the whole future is changed. The extreme weather conditions of the winter of 2017/18 disrupted the lives of many in the UK, causing untold accidents; we all have a story relating to that appalling weather.

Bereavement and life changing injuries affect people in different ways, something which I try to explore in ***The Accident***. For Hannah the accident brings physical pain as she struggles to carve out a new life coping with her injuries, and emotional pain, living with the tyranny of the 'what ifs' and battling with guilt. The ripples affect her family too, altering the future she'd always taken for granted. Joe, who loses his beloved wife, is at his lowest ebb but the ripples extend to his family too and become the catalyst for greed and hatred.

Grief can appear to break us, but perhaps also remake us. I've always admired those who channel their grief into something positive, and so Timothy[= Jones' parents become the example to us all. Refusing to allow their son's memory to die they decide to fulfil his dream and build a living monument to his lost life, to make his years on earth count for something. I so enjoyed writing their story; beauty from ashes!

If you enjoyed reading *The Accident*, I would be grateful for a review on **Amazon** and **Goodreads**. If you would like to offer your personal comments, please contact me on my **Facebook Author Page** or send a message through **Twitter.** You can also keep up to date with my writing projects on **my website**.

Gillian Jackson **gillianjackson.co.uk**

Sapere Books is an exciting new publisher of brilliant fiction and popular history.

To find out more about our latest releases and our monthly bargain books visit our website:
saperebooks.com

Printed in Great Britain
by Amazon

57449861R00116